CHIN CE

THE DREAMER
AND
THE ORACLE

African Books Network

THE DREAMER AND THE ORACLE by Chin CE
International Edition
  includes selested bibliography

For information address:
African Books Network
15803 S. Mapel Ave.
Gardena CA 90003
Email: handelbook@gmail.com

For Handel Books Limited
6/9 Handel Avenue
AI EBS Nigeria WA
Email: handelbook@yahoo.co.uk

Print Editions
Marketing and Distribution in the US, UK,
Europe, N. America (Canada),
and Commonwealth countries outside Africa by

 African Books Collective Ltd.
PO Box 721
Oxford OX1 9EN
United Kingdom
Email: orders@africanbookscollective.com

Front and Back Cover:
© African Books Network
ISBN: 978-9-7836-0368-4
An African Books Network Project
<http://www.handelbooks.africaresearch.org>

© Philip ???, 20??. All rights reserved. No part of this publication may be reproduced, stored in a retrieval system, or transmitted, in any form or by any means, electronic, mechanical, photocopying, recording or otherwise, without the prior written permission of the author and copyright holder.

Reprinted and reissued by
1 contains ??? strong
13(0)-08 March Avenue ???
London ??? ???

For the African Book ???
Unit ??? 24 Avenue ???
70-108 March ??? 8 ???
???

Marketing, Jacket & Content by the US, UK
and Company, ???, ??? Company
and Company, ???, ???, America

African Books Collective Ltd.

London ??? ???

British Library ??? in ???

Front and Back Cover
by Allan Books ???
ISBN 978-4-7836-8008
African Books Collective Program
Printed by ??? Publishing by ??? ??? ???

 **AFRICANBOOKS NETWORK**

African Books International Network

Since the year 2000 when we first launched our electronic program, we have converted our publications to eBooks for writers wishing to make the writing business a marketable venture in today's dynamic internet age. Now you can explore the opportunity of increased commercial traffic for your books through e-solutions aimed at aligning any remote region to the global network. Our e-program is easy and cost-effective and you can quickly reach several readers through downloads from online bookstores.

As the competitive book venture has ensured that publishing adopts the most resilient methods of pricing and service charges, African Books Network connects you to worldwide distribution schemes by which you track sales through online marketing networks around the world.

Contents

THE ORACLE

For Chinua Achebe (1930-2013)

"There is a drawn battle for the mind of this world. Some old men have been spreading the message of freedom and liberty, throwing words around, and quite a few are picking up these seeds in their heart.

"You will preach unity and faith, peace and progress, but read my lips: that four-footed creature draws from my mind, which controls behaviour on this soil with robotic precision.

"Negate and convict them, persuade them to repudiate their eternal worth; immobilise, demobilise and leave them stagnant within the contradictions of their doctrines and injunctions. Lead them to lie here at my feet.

"The great lie is their morality or lack of it; the more ignorant, the more loyal to my cause; the more fanatical and violent...

- Babul

Onku

*

I t was nearly noon but seemed to be morning yet. Koma's uncle
sat by his choice corner before the veranda of the house under
the shade of an ancient mango that now looked like a baobab tree
warming his legs by the hearth. He had finished a familiar one about
one of his travels round the world and was now contemplating his
pipe with a curious expression on his face. Komas and I pestered
him for another story.

"Onku, what can you tell me about the legend of Kongo twins,"
I ventured.

The harmattan blew a steady stream of cold chilly bursts that
scattered leaves and dusts. This season's was the strong type that
could dry the skin brittle and would freeze the bones if you let it. It
brought nostalgic memories of childhood, and carried even further
to some distant and forgotten periods in a dim past.

"Barw and Parw?" the old teacher frowned. His brows and
moustache were etched white. "That story is untold for the ear.
Sunu, son of my good friend, Evara," he called to me, "Why do you
want to know things that should not be told to young ears?"

"History, folklore, tradition," I feigned. "All these my class
teacher told us are very important knowledge."

"Surely, your memory has not failed you, Onku?" Komas shot
him a glance and we smiled furtively.

We both knew the trick to pull the leg of the grand master.
Wonder aloud if his memory was failing and you had him where
you wanted. Moreover Onku's travels round the world had made it
irresistible for him to share his stories with all who would listen.

He was a glorious old fellow, though well in his eighties now.

His face had an unnatural tinge behind the hardened marbled eyes that had looked fear and death in the face many times over. This great bird of our clan had known years of rare wisdom which the young, as he said, had yet to understand.

"Barwa and Parwa," he said again. "The big lie of history. One black like coal, the other fair like ripe pawpaw," he smiled to himself. It was as if a chapter of the story was lighting up in his memory. "After them, nobody could accept twins ever again in the whole of Kongo. Until Slessor came.

"Of course there are other versions," he acknowledged. "Some say they were not twins but brothers. Others that they were just friends, you know, 'five and six,' like you and Okoma here," he gestured to his great nephew who had a different kind of smile on his face. He was anticipating the old man.

Uncle or Onku -the way we called him- was actually the great uncle of Komas and, at his age, had become the oldest surviving member of the family as well as the entire clan of Omaha. It was said that Onku went to Cambridge but his unlettered grandfather, Aham, the great seer of Omaha, was the one who opened his many heads and placed the ancient knowledge and histories of the clan in them.

"Yes, I still have my memory intact," Onku warmed to the bait. "And one of you, maybe, will claim it when I pass on... that is, if the chickens will grow to look to cockerels for guidance. Ha! ha!"

We laughed with him.

"Oh yes," he went on gaily. "Only the old man knows the tune of a real tale. But first, you must make me my pipe, Oko," he commanded. "And you, Sunu, stir the fire to warm my bones."

"I'll get your golden herbs," Komas had that knowing smile on his face as he hastened to oblige while I gently brought the sticks and tinder to revive the hearth that warmed our uncle's bones.

Onku warmed to me with a gay chortle showing a whole pair of toothless gums save few brown and rusted molars. "Really," he teased, "you boys waste your time throwing cards these days. And you call that a game," he peered into my face with a foxy smile. "That's all you do in college these days?"

"No, we read books," I corrected. "Many books and quizzes, you know."

"Baa!" Onku snorted. "And what do those chap books tell ya! Blind as bats and leading their young to the ditch. Ha! If you learned at the feet of the oracle, you would come to know the true wisdom of mother Earth," he shuffled both feet reverently on the ground as if to emphasise Earth mother.

Presently Komas was back with Onku's pipe refilled, just the way the old fellow liked it, with a cloud of tobacco herbs in trail. Onku would tell you he had tended these herbs since his young days, even after his Cambridge, and before his travels; in fact, from time immemorial. Now he sucked luxuriantly from his pipe, sending out brilliant sparks of light accompanied with dull thuds of crackling seeds. His eyes glowed with pride as he puffed and let the smoke through his great nostrils and ears.

Then he blew straight to my face. Wincing, I made as if to cough and held my breath. This was the part he seemed to like for he gave a loud cackle of amusement at my discomfort. "You must smoke a pipe one day, boy," he told me. "Learn to open your head. Now where were we?" he asked.

"Barwa and Parwa" Komas reminded him.

"The big lie of history," I added.

"The tale is taboo, might turn your head when you hear it" he told me again. "And no," he raised his right hand; his brown and wizened index finger dug into my chest. I felt a sharp sting of pain from those puissant time-long talons.

"Only one survived: Baba Barwa who seized the life force of his twin and lived for seven whole generations," he went on speaking rapidly now: his was voice beginning to sound strange, like a tape in fast forward.

"Some say he never died but still lives, a phantom of a life, the sort that, rather than go on into the land of the ancients, falls back into the abyss, the darkness of this world, to become an incarnate of Enshu himself-

"Enshu," he smirked with near profound glee, "who never tires of the chase nor wearies of the hunt..." He paused for breath. His grey-haired nostrils and blackened lips were barely visible in the cloud that billowed from his pipe.

"And we, our land, my boy," his eyes, presently blood shot with mysterious gleams, dug into mine as his voice took an eerie note. I had a sudden sickening feeling in the pit of my stomach.

"We are the blighted quarry. Ha! Ha! Ha!"

My head was swelling, dizzy with vague, unearthly noises coming from Onku and some foggy dim visions that seemed to jog my body of memory alert.

Or numb?

Whatever the case, as it seemed just then, I must have been completely unprepared for what followed next.

Captives

*

uddenly I was running. I was running as fast as the wind, as fast as my thoughts, for then all else seemed lost in a blur; the entire world had fled with a rapidity that astonished even myself. Only a sound like the wind cooed sharply and furiously against my ears as I ran along a dusty road, blind and not looking.

I must have run for hours, maybe days. My breath was beginning to flail in short gasps. My lungs stung badly and my belly was a violent ache, like something was lodged sharply in my mid-section. I was dimly aware of lurching violently, reeling left and right, my legs sagging from underneath me. Finally I came down with a slow, weary slump, blacking out the hazy, fast receding world I fled from.

When my eyes opened again I found myself in a secluded corner of a long desert, sitting near a bare footstone among some dusty piles of rock. This was strange. Where was I?

It's Naigon, I realised, an arid area of the country so much talked about in the Kongo legends where great battles had taken place in human heads. Ahead stretched the desert and sand mounds of an endless sprawling wasteland where the sand and dusts swirled and danced in violent gyrations to wildly surging winds.

"To be free at last," I found myself muttering, although not knowing why I said that. Maybe it was the feeling of vastness and space in this region that impressed itself upon me as I found myself taking a rest to meditate upon the prospect of freedom from the blight upon our land. For everywhere around me was yawning poverty, and dry stone parches of sterility and scorch. The sun had become a never-setting glaze of terror. Its countenance seemed a fierce tinge of devilish vengeance upon this part of earth that seemed oblivious of all noble intents.

I began to thirst. Beads of perspiration had formed on my forehead and were dropping down my neck. I shut my eyes. I had a long history behind me, and a promising task ahead.

The wind was lashing like a violent and discarnate monster. Its gnarled, deathly hand seemed to lace over my head; a sense of foreboding gripped me as it hovered ever so near. Then came the howling of greyhounds on the trail of a lone prey in panic. I was seeing images of terror, and I knew, somehow, they were projected by my pursuers in the matrix of thought. I could even imagine noises of cackling and dancing around huge earthenware filled with magic grog. And fear seized my heart. The muscles of my eyes were hurting from the strain of keeping them tightly shut from the monstrous spectres that flew in my imagination.

I had come a long way from a past that now threatened even in this solitary dryness to pull me by the ears. It was a great effort to keep still in that terror and not let out a yell and bound away to any ever place. Sit still, shut it tight, and do not give away your hiding place with even a whisper, I told myself.

But then, out of the glistening emerged a head like that of a hound. His teeth were barred, his lips curled in a snarl. He was hunched almost double as he sniffed the air. His paws, hung limply from a gnarled hairy chest, made careless patterns on the ground. Then our eyes met and he gave out a long growl of vicious temper. I recognised him immediately. My kinsman waB! That dreaded messenger of Babul and chief of his staff of minions!

"So there you are," he barked in that taut manner of his liege himself. "You thought you could escape the power of my arms, didn't you?"

Curiously my fear had lasted for one brief spell, one fleeting paralysing moment. And then it was gone, made way for the contempt I had for the likes of Babul's guards that were now emerging from beneath the sands of the land.

"I have come a long way," I replied, feeling a surge of strength welling from within. Surely, this new wave of energy could not be mine, thought I. It was as if some higher power had quickly impressed through my head, arms, neck and fingers the power to fight at this final moment where I had my back to a wall of sand. And all I needed was to stretch a long and defiant arm that would summon the forces of liberty to an explosive battle with my captors. But I also saw in another light that this struggle was between me and a severe force I had not quite understood. So the balance of power tilted against me.

"I have come a long way, waB," I warned again. "I am not going back."

The beast in him was cast in the character of his lord. waB believed himself prince as his master was king, and this was since the dimwit was made daemon for his stiff loyalty in the fold. I could now remember how my voice to free the innocents trapped in the tower of lies had risen in the assembly, and how the tag of renegade was strapped on my chest in blackmail. Now waB had summoned a large mass to back him in his bid to grab back a rebellious soul to the fold, and there was nothing to do but follow them, or fight back.

There was too much to bear and too much to take for granted. Their masks would haunt anyone, visages of terror and darkness, and here too, in the blazing desert, one must strain and struggle to be free of the sham that cluttered the mind, and then win a victory that ensured our survival, indeed, our purpose of coming to earth.

All these thoughts raced through my mind like an intense downpour, and they were pouring from some source from deep within me although I knew not its origin.

"We are here to take you back," waB said again, with very little patience, adding finally, "to where you belong."

"So you have come to tell me where I belong," I retorted angrily but with that strange feeling of peacefulness within. Perhaps another unseen guide had given me calm, silent composure to face these hounds, I mused, even as waB's eyes turned angry flashes of blood red. "Don't be silly," he snapped, "You belong to your duty, back where you fled. Now let's go. You are enough disgrace to your fellows. Baba was there; he came personally in the midst of the congregation to witness your call..."

"Stop! Stop that, you moron!" I yelled with vehemence. "You parrot too much nonsense from that murderous tyrant. Surely waB, that kind of life is not for us at all. We must stop; we must quit that den or lose our selves to hopeless evil."

waB only wrung his neck leftward and rightward, and then leant forward with a leering grin. "I knew you won't give easy," his visage changed as he straightened his muzzle. "Take him!" he thundered. His eyes were now his lord's firework, the smell of his breath, straight in my face, like dragon belching. The rest of the beasts who had lain in the background now began to emerge from both sides, eyes aflame, lips curled and parted, fangs barred; their measured stealthy walk, their single determination exuded from the tormenting power of meanness and violence for which waB and his league were famous.

So this was it. The moment of the great battle! The war to hit back and assert your spirit unfettered had now begun.

But a strange thing happened just then.

I burst into laughter.

The Proposal

*

They had carried me without further resistance for I had laughed and laughed all the way.

My sense of sight, sound and smell was profound. It tapped into luxuriant planes were all things glowed bright and beautiful. Even the sun had receded to a wondrous twilight of glowing beauty. There was the softest soporific hand in the air that melded with heavenly music and brought only more laughter to the heart. It was a strange sense of humour that tickled the spirit and tempered the will for battle.

And so I had let them carry me, offering no resistance, curiously, it did seem a little to me.

I was still beside myself with glee when I stood, irreverent and unbowed, before the great conqueror of souls and nations.

"I have enjoyed the ride through sinking sands and here in your dungeon, O lord, master and king of the fringe," I saluted. "Now what doth the rogue want of me?"

Babul shot a disapproving look at his chief of staff. "Hounds!" he scowled, "you gave him too much of that gas, waB!"

"You wanted him intact, Sire," waB explained. "We could have hurt him badly. He was ready to fight till the death."

Not that I would have won the fight anyway, I told myself. It could have been easy to knock out a few; but the rest? Well, I didn't have to find out, which seemed wise enough. I had often insisted that one man could win a fight against the crowd; it didn't always have to be one way for the mindless mob. But in this case, seeing through the whole drama was like the sheep that would bleat once and just stare, telling herself it is the bleary eye that sees through the foolishness of men. You see, 'let's ride along and see' is freedom you grant a maniac. Your present resistance gone, you watch the fool with the rope edging to hang himself. Those were the thoughts that humoured me as I let them carry me across the desert and into the presence of this lord of the den.

"Give him a tranquilizer," Babul ordered. "I won't have him talking to me in this manner!"

Rough hands grabbed me and led me out. They threw me into a room and stuffed a lot of stuff in my body. And I was instantly helped to a blissful passage in unconsciousness.

An Argument

*

After what must have been days when I came round, I found myself again in his presence. The great Babul was dressed like a warrior as he paced the floor. His hands were folded behind his back. His huge black and red drape was hung down his shoulder sweeping the floor and covering a pair of hinds ensconced in black leather boots.

"I brought you back," he started with mild, condescending friendliness... and a pause.

"So that you can fully appreciate the seriousness of the task before you," his blood-shot eyes bore into mine.

"And the enormity of my power!" he spat violently.

He let a few seconds pass. Then he spoke again. He was persistent, and ruthless. "Prodigal, there is no leaving the service of your lord in search of a short cut. Which is better, to flee from my wrath or come willingly into my service with all pleasure guaranteed."

"Pleasure?" I said meekly. It was deceptive meekness for its lack of strength and want of resolve to run the race with the wolves whose sinews always rippled to serve and be rewarded for their efforts. This lord must be so vain as to think only he had all the cunning of his negative mind hanging on the iroko tree.

A brief smile lit the face of the monster. A patronising smile a general would give his loyal officer. Then it was gone.

"At least you catch up fast enough. You have been with the prophet, and seen my power at work throughout this country. You have also been with these people for twenty five years now. All this was to let you into the dynamics of my laws, to rule the minds of men with the power I have given you."

I was silent and wondering. Scenes of the wretchedness of our lives, our country, all our reckless past began to light the fogged screen of my mind. I recognised the images conjured before me but they were arid reminders of failure, and more failure, graft hanging plastic shield of imaginary greatness and migl labours of their heroes.

In their stead began to gather, unconsciously, thoughts and subtle impressions of what must be done with the lessons unfurled, knowledge that must be gathered with a clarity that stunned the conscious mind, things that were not found nor discovered in the abruptness of latent guilt over a botched past. The Emperor did not seem to like this.

"There he goes again," he complained, "broking your thoughts. I don't like your thoughts when I see them... they are so heretical... not the allegiance you swore to me on Easter night."

"Mayor killed Zahara," I burst out. "Your man of God! A mindless murderer. And you want me to be like him..."

"Watch your tongue my boy," Babul puffed. "Questioning is no sign of loyalty at all."

But I was undaunted.

"You preside over a moral fury, a naked irresponsible abuse of power!"

"Of course, being the lord, I am entitled to my fury. Don't forget the two are inseparable, power and anger -or fury, whatever you call it. The fury of my power rules the mind of the world, must rule your own too, for your whole benefit."

"Our benefit indeed!" I returned. "You could not even protect the lives... of Zahara and her mother. Lives brutally taken. The life you never gave in the first place."

"A few lives must be taken to further my cause," Babul gestured with an indifferent shrug of his huge mane of shoulders. "Those two are inconsequential."

"Inconsequential!" I exploded. "You see, our lives are inconsequential before you," I shouted to no one in particular. "Where is justice if your cause must fizzle the lives of others any time you wish."

"Wrong," Babul snapped his jaws. "You make endless sacrifices for higher cause. Think of the classic sacrifice: your saviour. Some still drink his blood at sacrament. Isn't that rather barbarous? Your rebellious mind should tell you that these are offertory for divine succour -another lesson in the course of your ministry."

"Zahara and her mother were not willing sacrifice," I went on as if he hadn't even spoken. "I believed in you because I thought you help people find the way of light."

"Young fellow!" Babul replied in a raised voice, "death shall serve my cause when it will... but enough of the long talk. Go and make disciples of the faith. Teach how to put money in their hands and make them happy -the happiness you rejected by shunning the priesthood of my kingdom."

"We are not all maggots crawling for dirty bills, my liege. How wrong, how disgusting of you!" I made a face.

"And who are you to determine wrong from right?" Babul yelled impatiently. "You carry out my orders, it's simple enough. Who ever queries the injunctions of the realm?" his voice lowered menacingly. "Now listen, earthworm, I am getting rather tired of this cat-and-mouse with you. In this job, never ask questions or even think with your mind, which is mine by the power of my hand. I do the thinking; you are to act my wish.

"You execute my order. There never were two masters in a realm, or you might well begin to question my authority -the highest rebellion in the scrolls."

"That's what I've always wanted," I replied with equal measure of irreverence, "to know who the hell you are!"

"Blasphemy!" he muttered and made to stop his ears with his claws. "But we will deal with this later."

The Oracle

The unwilling quarry and the ruthless hunter. I knew this was going to be a long and hopeless argument.

Last Prophet

*

"Now here's the new deal, countryman," said Babul to me several hours, or several days later, I could not count the period of my captivity. Tired, hungry and abandoned, I beheld my captor this time like a true man of God. He was indulgently reclined in elegant regalia of white trousers and overcoats to match. Even his stockings, shoes and necktie were all impeccably white. Babul's exotic taste not adding his wining and dining was open secret among his select initiates.

"You shall not be deacon anymore; you shall be the prophet of the millennium."

I gave a start of surprise. Actually from deacon to prophet was indeed a miraculous transformation even for a renegade like me. But what had just come from this barrel of neck, this robust set of cheeks, and awfully indulged lips, was all in character. Promotion to anywhere was not by merit. It came as special favours determined by the caprice of the lord himself. I could imagine what this arrangement did to the hierarchy all jostling for attention and recognition. But then I was laughing again.

"Is this another miracle?"

The beast showed his teeth in an angry snarl, the creature underneath his stylish appearance wanting to tear to open. But he won't let it yet.

"You shall teach them the faith," he went on, ignoring my bemusement. "Your duty will be to gather them, many more disciples and masses who will be looking up to you. They are groping in their minds for a few explosive tickets to health, wealth and power, and you have the tricks. Tricks are necessary if you must gain a sizeable following."

But I was silent, which to Babul must have meant my consent, for he then adjusted himself more comfortably in his grand seat ornamented with mirrors. Copious silvery lining trapped the flaming red lights in the room and threw angry fireworks around the corners as he whispered conspiratorially to me.

"You know, I was going to add unto you the legacy of Pastor Chris. He did his bit very well and now he's gone, blown up by a disgruntled church member, isn't that rather sad?

"They said he preached too many fearful sermons," he continued. "Well, now, those chilly waves of fear among the flock was power, you know.

"But I understand you want to teach peace, *asalam,* and whatever. You must add to them the comfort of a permanent state of witlessness. I will explain:

"There is a drawn battle for the mind of this world. Some old men who refuse to die -those compromisers of the first heaven who can't just keep their mouths shut- have been spreading their message of freedom and liberty, just like you do: throwing words around, and quite a few are picking up these seeds in their heart.

"You will preach unity and faith, peace and progress, but read my lips: that four-footed creature draws from my mind which controls behaviour on this soil with robotic precision.

"Negate and convict them, persuade them to repudiate their eternal worth; immobilise, demobilise and leave them stagnant within the contradictions of their doctrines and injunctions. Lead them to lie here at my feet.

"The great lie is their morality or lack of it; the more ignorant, the more loyal to my cause; the more fanatical and violent...

"No, no I can see you are getting pretty confused," Baba waved his hands in the face of his silent captive -me- who watched his every movement like a stalking eagle.

"Now let's put it this way. What are those other faces of peace and harmony but dissension, violence and war; of love and service but competition and hate? Mine shall overrun or contribute to overturn the affirmative for ascendancy of every mediocrity within the entire fabric of existence: simple quantum leveller.

"Your founding fathers did the same. Others are doing it now. We are the hydra of every age on this soil.

"And all I am saying is lead -lead them along; carve a ready following. But teach these in verses and that great singing and dancing for which you are famous. And, with the powers I shall add to it, you become the youngest prophet to dazzle the hunger of the age."

"But 1 will tell you again, young man, to beware of sabotage: Why seek ye knowledge beyond your grip?" he leaned forward and shoved white-gloved claws in my face. "Now your lord cannot preside over the sabotage of his powers, can he?"

I inwardly recoiled realising that by knowledge he had actually meant truth. But cutting into his loathsome monologue, I blurted out: "I can't!"

My words seemed to jar him. He started briefly. And then the dangerous gleam appeared in his eyes again.

"You can't? You mean rebel once more against me?" Babul growled. "Then surely damnation will be your judgement. Even as your father, I will sit and preside over the radius of the brimstone that will consume you forever. You must understand, boy. East or west. North or south, the show must go on, whether you want it or not."

There was sudden silence.

His was an ominous threat. Mine was in contemplation of the complex paradox that gave rise to such a nightmare of human imagination. Or was it silence from my own confounded grip by a titan who bestrode the human mind with his awesome power and abuse of it?

I sought to go further than I did, to recapitulate my experience, to reveal the identity of this beast and the methodology upon which its tyranny was founded and nourished. Beyond even that, I sought to know more.

I was pressed to know its origins and the many faces it wore to destabilise nations, uproot souls and weed every resistance in men, women and children. I sought to know how it managed to succeed in turning all of us into living walking dead or cuddly cats that would meow forever in the bodies of priests and mayors...

The effort must have triggered some force in me, an energy that, in the blatant negated presence of my oppressor, added to my own hunger and tiredness, proved too much for my human body.

Babul was saying, "but first, we need a revolution," and was motioning for attention with his index finger when I fell into a deep and welcome sleep.

Swords Arise!

*

A moment would often seem like a blink of an eye especially when something unusual was about to happen. That was how I found myself among the rebels of Naigon dunes fighting the tyranny of a mad legion of vampires.

In a blink of an eye.

In those brief nanoseconds of mind flights, my search led me through the revolutionary years when we all picked the sword in riot and defence of democracy in the city. I found myself among many angry groups thirsty for blood; even the fiery, fanatical mob of religious devotees and defenders of God were not left out. But that was not it...

I was standing on a level plane overlooking the desert sands of the three lands. Below were the dune rocks, barely visible, covered by years of dust and grime, a remote desert region which had had been the quarantine of the successive vampires that ravaged the land since the time of its birth. From within the seclusion of their quarters they had looted the land's wealth leaving its earth sun-scorched and barren, and the dunes people poor, hungry and desperate.

The wind was blowing furious sand storms as if warning anyone who cared to listen that an event of portentous nature was about to happen on this land. And in the far distance away from where I was looking for the sign in the raging wind, it seemed the stair of rock mounds covered with many years of grime and sand began to heave before my very eyes. Now tense in mind, disturbed by appearances that seemed my own making, though not entirely mine, I watched excitedly and somewhat disinterestedly too.

I remembered squatting low, as in my childhood days, my hands under my chin, but then I was staggering to full length when the mountains surrounding the mass of sand and rock heaved with a loud, deafening noise. Then followed a gigantic flame that burst upon the land like volcano. Its sheer radioactive power sent me flying instantly in many jagged directions. And as soon as I landed on one place and looked around in wonderment, there were people.

Or rather heads! Flat heads and cone heads were pounding out of the roaring mountain. Heads in kerchiefs and hats and turbans were tumbling crazily over the dusts and sands in propulsions so irregular and so destructive. And what had they in their hands?

"Swords and spears!"

It was him again.

"Today is your lucky day, young man," Babul greeted airily. "For you meet me as king of the ancient kingdom of Musanga and the one in the head of every man woman and urchin."

So this long-legged creature had been here all along was all I thought; now realising this must be a scene of his own weaving. He had on gaudy attire with all the shine and steel of epaulettes.

But I had no time for chit chats as I raced, or rather wobbled, down the sandy decline, hobbling and gurgling for breath, falling and somersaulting, until coming to find my feet among the mass of cone and flat heads. It was then I heard their collective voice: a chilling monotonous chant of war. Sufficiently in panic now, nevertheless eager to find out more, I caught a grip on a huge trunk of leg and yanked. "What's happening?" I asked.

"Get off!" the owner smacked wildly. I parried the blow but came to sprawl full length on my face, licking the dust and grit and all.

The flames appeared to have simmered down almost as soon as they began, leaving belching of embers and curling tongues of grey smoke. And the people stretched before me were a massive colonnade of human heads rolling along the dust of the earth. The chant of violence had lowered almost inaudibly into a fiendish monotone. Yet how hungry and lean they looked. A drawn and tired herd without a leader, I thought.

But even as I looked anew with a growing mixture of horror and fascination, one or two heads among the hundreds proceeded to merge -two heads and three bodies for a leader. A huge and bloated figurine stepped out from the masses like a heavyweight champion to combat.

There was a brief silence.

Then the crowd roared in the wildest and roudiest greeting I ever heard or saw. Their noise became the crescendo of seismic rumbling. And from within the roaring came the massive fury of a weak, hungry and diabolical people.

"We must to Aso!" the champion yelled. And they repeated after him in self-same monotones.

"Down with the enemy!"

"Down with our enemy!

'Kill the vampires!"

"Kill the vampires!"

Thus with swords and arrows and some junk and scraps of metal raised over their heads, the crowd lunged forward towards the rock stairs that led to the abode of the president and his league of blood suckers.

From the blur of faces I picked a familiar one. It was one of my colleagues shot in the back at the national stadium on June 12. And I was thinking: What on earth was he doing here among the living dead? His hands were flying wildly and one could even see the veins that stood like cords of rivulets from his neck.

"To Aso," we yelled again, this time feebly as if under a strange hypnotic influence. The world seemed unreal but it didn't matter as we tumbled along to bare a thousand grudges at the seat of power.

Soon we were joined by women and hawkers and touts from the streets of the crowded city. Anything seemed possible here. I found myself leaping high in excitement as every one threw hands into the air and caught a weapon.

The Oracle

"To the Rock!"

It didn't take long, however, before everything began to fall to pieces. Not one or two, but the whole mass were tumbling down like little rocks from a precipice. One leap again, and I landed on top of a skyscraper. There I hung for dear life to survey the progress below and study the next line of action.

Babul joined me in a new revolutionary guise. He appeared very tall like a ghost-world phantom and also wore a cone for a head, while the masses were being mowed down like grass before the lawn mower even as they lashed and dived in frantic flights to safety. Something in the soup had turned it sour. There was confusion, more than ever recorded in the whole of the dry, strangulated land. Grenades were flying through the air to explode in blinding fireworks. Ghastly volleys kept bursting right in the middle of the crowd below. And the tanks -actually bulldozers- rolled diabolically in pursuit, spitting fire, grenades and bombs as hooded soldiers in head gears mopped up the action with machine guns, blazing a trail of blood and death and cutting their way through the clutter of the fallen and dying.

"The bastards!" I exclaimed.

Babul was by my side grinning widely, his four eyes agleam with excitement. "I told you I'm in the head of every one. After today, the whole of Naigon will come to me; they will call me Baba, father and mighty warrior; they will plead that I put an end to all their misery," he chuckled with a delight that was incomprehensible to my senses.

"This is shameful," was all I could utter.

"Shameful indeed," Babul concurred.

"Monstrous," I ejaculated.

"Monstrous? Yes."

"Fools!"

"Save I the King," he laughed.

"Morons!"

"Morons all of you, yes."

I didn't bother to swear further because his inane repetitions and turning everything I said back to me were getting on my nerves. I was blinded by the same emotion that was akin to the madness of the human world. "The people are nearly finished," I stared, stupefied. But Babul was searching the sky above his head. And that was when I heard another sound.

"What is that?" I looked up with fright.

Tanks!

Flying junks of hardware were spitting torrents of hell just above our heads. The sky scrapers were crumbling.

I leapt down... down over the hills and trees, over the volcano and the rumbling and destruction below; and picking a lone cactus far and safe from the blood scent underneath I folded into my wings in a dejected cry. "They are finishing the nation, one and all!"

Babul appeared presently, laughing excitedly, his fist clenched, proud and satisfied in his great knowledge and power.

"My boys are back," he exclaimed, pumping his fists in the air. "General St Bach, hear him!"

The air was now filled with the clanging of martial beats. A high, excited voice bawled to us as Babul adjusted the little radio he held in his palms.

"We cannot stand aside and watch the the rise of indiscipline in our polity. Civil disobedience is a heinous crime anywhere in the world and it is our duty to restore law and order."

"Order," Babul croaked with laughter. "They are restoring order... come," he pulled me and we fell headlong and down again. How I feared we might crash to death below the gorges filled to the brim with destruction.

I landed on the grass with a jar that brought the taste of bile on my lips. But I was unhurt. I was never to hurt in this play of nightmare within the human mind.

Instead I found myself among another angry group thirsty for more blood; a fiery, fanatical mob of religious devotees and defenders of God.

"Death!" they yelled, "to infidel!"

"Death to aliens!"

In another blink of an eye they hacked a thousand and one of their own to death. The blood seemed to have gone to their heads for anyone just had to point: "This is a stranger, kill!" And they hacked him down.

We soon burst into a fenced courtyard that I would never fail to recognise even in the maze of the nightmarish world I was now living. It was the old government house our uncle had built. Babul was leading them, captain and commander of the whole garb of masses in dirty flowing overalls. "Come on!" he waved to everybody. The crowd roared and billowed after him.

It was easy to barge through the door. The gate keepers had scampered away at the first sound of noise. In the wide and richly furnished floor of the great duplex that Uncle Jack built, Babul motioned to wait. He flew up, up the staircase and was back in a second. Then he motioned up toward the bedroom quarters.

I raced past him and past everyone and landed inside the bedroom.

Jack Lugard lay on the bed, and there was another, his lady: she smelled imperial, her nose pointed imperial, and she wore a brace.

Flora!

She first gave me a blank stare, and then let out a piercing scream, her brace falling from her teeth. Bending forward to the rescue, I was feeling a strange pity, the pity the mob would not have for her right there and then if they had her. But a shot rang past my ear and brushed her slightly down the middle. The couple froze in a sickly pigment of grey.

"My God," Jack groaned to his wife. "What have we done?"

"Death to imperialist!" came the rumbing below.

That galvanised me to action.

"Quick! Into the toilet!" I shoved them both with a violent push and slammed the door just as the captain appeared, guns blazing.

"Death to infidel!"

"They're not here," I shouted.

"Search everywhere," he bawled back.

They searched, under the bed, pulled down the blinds, ransacked the wardrobes, and emptied the clothes in them.

"In the kitchen! Search the toilet!" came the command of the captain.

I had a feeling that Jack must not die there today. I prayed Oh God, let this man must not die here today. And inside the toilet chamber I knew Jack was praying desperately too for a second chance.

Babul slashed and cut the air left and right, coming to an abrupt stop halt before the door where I leaned to regain my breath. He just stood there gibbering some monstrous mantra and waving a wand in the air.

"Behold your prize all ye faithful," he waved.

Money! Money! Money!

And that was it.

The rest of the mob, crawling through the door, was now giant clusters of wriggling maggots. Clumsily, in their hurried surge to barge in all at once, they wriggled.

Babul released ungainly volleys of gunshots here and there while still muttering his abracadabra. His voice had turned a coarse preternatural growling: "Behold your prize!"

The excited wrigglers tore the door to shreds and a horrendous struggle began, a fight of fists and claws with which they grabbed the bills from one another's hands and yelled curses in the air.

Soon the room was filled with violent throaty oaths as everyone grabbed and grabbed more and more precious-than-life note bills from any hand that held them. Any hand.

For a second I stood confounded, and then suddenly began to reel and stagger dangerously. Someone had nearly knocked the breath of life from me while I was gaping, someone cursing and snarling. I cursed and kicked back hard. Then I blinked awake, flicking my eyes around the darkness of a lonely apartment. Where was I?

The sweat poured from my face and neck, drenching my pillow: my eyes darted back and forth like a caged rat desperate for a way, a way out of the prison of our lives, out of that cold clammy realization that my whole world was reeling wildly and going to pieces.

Babul was winning!

Jaws

*

I t's been several weeks since the offensive that was launched to bring down the rebellion of the dunes, our rebellion from taskmasters who drained the life and blood of the land. Babul had tried all methods to change me to his side: dangled the carrot and wielded the stick. When all didn't seem to work very much, he kept prodding the flock from the ministry of Maloo to visit, pray for me and be sure that I was alright.

But I wasn't fooled. I knew these people were merely keeping tabs of their own service to their master. They believed him to be everywhere and everything they could never hope to become. Babul worked hard at playing sorcery and omnipresence in a gross material sense. Many times I could feel his presence, smell his breath over my hair and, once, I could swear I felt his cold nose touch the nape of my head.

Well, I was truly disturbed.

How could I be the only one who knew this entity for what he was? And how was I to rid myself of this creature whose devotees ought to have known and loathed as much as I did now? He had everybody praying to him everywhere you went, just as he had gloated. He was right on that count, though. Fridays the mosques were filled, then the churches to the brim Sundays, for Baba, father and mighty warrior, to deliver them from the evil in the world.

The evil he had created for us, I laughed mirthlessly. Ah, that was religion. All things to the glory of the father and mighty who delivered his people from the enemy. And now with the revolution and bloodshed of the new regime, there was no dull moment for the millions of believers that thronged the three lands of Naigon.

Millions like me.

Sometimes I had the subtle feeling that the actual struggle was happening inside us and not the outside scenes that we saw daily with our physical eyes. On that score I badly need the help of someone who knew better the things I felt, and who probably felt more deeply the things I knew.

But loneliness itself had become my lot. I found no one who knew the things I knew. Nobody saw the visions I saw. These remained my bad dreams, the nightmares of a hundred demons of Baba's handiwork dancing to some percussion in my head. And as if that was not enough punishment, a terror was coming full circle in the matrix of our world, a strange terror that came from somewhere else and had everyone in line. Each wave it blew would paralyse the faculty, distort the vision and make everyone yield helplessly to the joker in the field of minds.

For a long time I was too terrified of the consequences of this war in the head to act on my vow to find the source of Baba's powers. How could you when nobody in the whole world seemed to know what was happening behind the daily mystique of survival battles that held them in awe. Everyone was afraid to question the very basis of the doctrines of faith and state, those stories and platitudes that assailed our ears daily and weekly, and dulled our spirit into mere fleshly walking zombies. But for me, to die, a slave of any following, unable to take back control of my mind, would give no meaning to my life's passage from this sphere. Something was telling me that the fears that spurred us to ultimate immolation were all that this lord of the out-realm needed to reign over us. It was fear that drove us to the altar to join other folks to knock our heads like lizards and sing and clap our hands as in kindergarten. And when greed donned the bloody garb it was ready to hit the streets to kill and loot in the wild wanton nature of the very same beast with another face. Yeah, that was politics, of course.

These thoughts usually came to me when I kept steady on the quest, but again, a veil would black out efforts to find out more leaving only the eerie loneliness that came with the knowledge. It seemed to me that we had been far too terrorised to face ourselves, which meant to confront the monster lurking at the edge of the mind, grab him by the jaws and throw him down the precipice for the good of the world. In my head fear and desperation rang the moral litany of every act of cowardice that screamed, 'don't be the odd man out!' But wasn't it exactly such fear that turned back the wheel of any progress, bid you refuse to face your self and had the devil himself right in the front corner of your own driveway?

So my fear had remained there with me drowning the quest till that morning when I woke up and sought refuge in the company of old friends.

In my mind I could still see them, Billy Bill and Komas and I, as we used to spend the days playing poker and wearing faces. It was the ultimate trick of the world. With Bill you were the fool who neither knew what to do next nor could ever remember clearly what he had done before. A loyal dog he was to his fun and habits, no questions asked.

And with Komas?

You only winked, laughed and smiled even when the situation called for anything other than winking, laughing and smiling. 'Your face is your mask,' he would say, 'and you must wear many faces to play the game of the world and beat the system.'

Beat the system indeed! We had made a team of poker and skirt chasers then with our art. But who cared for those things these days? With separate interests friendships would drift. They went for their own gut frills and I was alone. Hopefully, our interests would meet again at some indistinct point in earthly time -or that was what I thought.

It seemed like yesterday when they planned to observe what was going on live at the conference of nationalities. The new government had restored the congress and approved sovereign conference. But it was trying to make nonsense of the entire jaw-jaw project by filling the slots of representatives with their own nominees. So some brave nationals were going to protest this at the venue. Now, *Protest*, which used to be our right, and carried a great ring of excitement, had all been forgotten in this part of the world. Poor woman, this *Protest*, someone had once exclaimed. Today she would be remembered and her lost glory restored: the glory of dissent that was the crown of all the odd and oppressed people of the world.

And so to the venue we went.

But then it was sad to see only motley pressmen and women photographing the official dignitaries of the occasion. A handful of what would look like *Protest* herself stood limply by the corner of the door showing placards which effectively barred them from entering the hall even as mere observers like us.

The congress was a large building strangely built like a mosque in the heart of the capital city and filled with silhouettes of conferencing heads, hats, caps, turbans, head-ties and wigs. Here painted faces, hairy furs, beefy imbeciles, downright orgres and the very worst of the dead century who shaped the affairs of state in their passionate intensities. Facing them was a group of speakers who sat behind a long table. It was covered with a stained green and white cloth whose white had long turned brown with dirt and hasty washing. What appeared to be a bouquet of flowers stood in the centre of the table. It occurred to me the flowers looked rather ill at ease among the humans wearing their face masks.

There were loud bickering going on outside the hall. The protest was gathering.

Then how very apt, I thought.

I had come to join the outside noise in the hope to muffle and drown the noise inside my head. Or better put, here was I running away from Babul and his endless chatter, and yet the more I ran, the more he seemed to hang around like a leech. For right there, in the middle of the hall, where the hawing and chattering was in full swing, Baba too had come to the congress of baboons.

He had on a dissembling robe worn like a priestly dalmatic and a black belt around his waist. His smile was peaceful only when you did not look into his eyes to see the deadness in them. I could only stare in dumbfoundment. Bill had looked at me and said, "Man, you look like you *seen* a ghost!" He didn't know how right he was.

"I defy your diagnosis," Baba gloated noisily in my ear. "Even the witches of Europe are puzzled at the immensity of my powers. And they have remained loyal servants.

"I brought you here to learn a few things from my servants. You have only to observe and listen, and the reward shall be yours to have."

I cleared my throat and threw a furtive glance behind to see if anyone else was staring. The father-warrior of the world could be very loud and audible.

But the cynosure of eyes at that time was the one called the chief press secretary or cps of the new regime, a.k.a. the interpreter-of-the-word. Rough-bearded and loud-talking, he had won many prizes for his loyalty to past regimes. Now his duty was to relate government policy to the hearing and understanding of every man and child of the new nation.

He was quite adept at the trade, contriving and summing up all that the speakers had said, always in relation to government position.

"There sits the prophet Maloo, my favoured son," Baba motioned with his snout, "to whom you are apprenticed in the magic of holy ministries.

"And there half awake and dozing is his royal highness of the golden teeth and million dollar regalia, the great Alewa Baraka."

"Yes," I replied with several nods to this luring and goading in the promises of worldly splendour. "I know the people's hero and father of the lords of the tribe," I added dryly.

Who didn't know the shameful history of this country's unity and faith?

"I can also see Colonel Samba, representative of General St Bach, the new strongman of Naigon," I continued.

"Samba it was who led the bloody putsch against Salami from the mid west and he it was who shot the old man in the head, not so?"

Babul nodded proudly.

But there was a nondescript old fellow simply called teacher whose method was to contest the easy resolution of unity and faith, peace and progress with questions and musings. Now this was the sort I admired, the sort that annoyed everyone else, particularly the cps, even more particularly, Babul himself.

The interpreter was up on his feet. As cps, he was saying, it was his job to correct a very misleading notion against the government by the teacher.

"I find it impertinent," he fondled his tie with pride, "that when all the important voices of the land have spoken in the same voice..."

There were muffled noises rising in the hall, whether in support of the mere commotion outside or in opposition to his talk it was not clear. He broke off for effect, and then continued in a streaming marathon.

"Even our Muslim and Christian leaders here saw no bleak sign in the horizon of our great nation as this man supposes. They agree that God has a glorious plan for this great nation -a unanimous resolution without a single minus or equal.

"Here today, everyone is full of praises for the noble achievements of the general in the relative short time of his government and all over the nations there are many prayers by all to God to allow His steward to go on without opposition.

"All, except, probably, one dissenting voice among us -a tale bearer!" he gestured at the nondescript gentleman seated imperturbably among the speakers.

There was uproar from the hall and a point of order was shouted asking the cps to mind his language. As the undaunted interpreter waved for silence his rough beards appeared to quiver remorselessly.

"I suppose to call him tale bearer rather than story teller is all the same anyway. A teacher is a storyteller because he teaches by his stories. But we came here to separate facts from fiction, and that is what teacher has not done," the cps was beginning to rasp like a dying bee that had left its sting on the neck of her victim.

"This man dares to link our great leadership with monstrosity, criminality and a whole load of mediocrity. Ladies and gentlemen," the interpreter banged both fists on the table in a fit of bad temper. "This is madness of the first order!"

And then my lips curled with scorn.

It was not for the teacher, as Babul sooner noted. My disdain at that very moment was directed to the interpreter. For the antic of shooting down one lone voice with a hundred drones was all too familiar in the dirty politics of the nation. Babul cleared his throat and teased. "You are getting worked up to the wrong in direction."

It puzzled me how this ghost followed my mind like clockwork. He knew I had begun to see in the teacher what many of us should become, maybe with a little courage. The teacher tickled a dormant seed to life, to a new eye that saw the favourite masks of these fellows with increasing disdain. Now as he rose and spoke even more fearlessly, I felt his words yanking off the hood of a criminal to reveal the jaws of the ugly visage behind a dangerous game. There it was, the words seemed to tell me. This was total mind control. For the glory of an evil that masqueraded as human material goodness in every corner you turned your eyes.

And Babul was aware of this awakening, this rousing effort to discover how everything here had been arranged to control all our behaviour. We should all be true teachers, I was thinking; bold, fearless, free from the anger of the ego lord when his blind patterns were being impeached by clearer vision.

"A useless effort," he sneered. "Soon you may also start to wonder if you are no just ordinary mortal... you can never rise above your little self, above your past... The servants of Baba do not stand aside from the popular train like your teacher is doing.

"Remember your bond with the masses. Now, that is power beyond compare. You cannot now disdain them that you loved and vowed to die fighting their cause, can you?"

"I made no such vow," I countered loudly.

A number of faces had turned in my direction. But how could I care a dog shit now?

May Day! May Day!

*

"Wow! Take it easy," Babul began, sensing my protest. I knew he was up to more tricks whenever he said 'take it easy' in that condescending and conciliatory manner of his. "Let's regress a bit now," he continued; "let's go a little further back in time, not very far from here.... It's still the hoary eighties. Surely you remember May Day.

"You were running, actually fleeing, from those canister balls. They stung painfully in your lungs, but you ran, along with others, fleeing like rabbits, paws, tails and all.

"Yes, you are there now. And those balls thudded everywhere. Your eyes followed the pair of canvas shoes that seemed to flit noiselessly across the ground..."

Listening to his droning, with my mind considerably dulled, made his invasion an easy drill. My brain was like a malfunctioned clock working slowly backward, then reeling dizzily anti clockwise.

My body went numb as the legs in canvas shoes my eyes were following suddenly leapt high up and landed on the dust. I tried to jump but too late! I came down with a heavy thud. A canister hit my head. The fumes hissed directly under my nose. Another. Then another.

I scrambled to my feet, lungs suffocating, my eyes stinging, my face smarting painfully. In the haze, I caught a glimpse of a blue uniform edging after me. Mad dogs! I spat and coughed violently. It felt like hell as the canister balls rained down.

Dazed, I ran harder. My lungs were threatening to burst. Then I burst through the thicket. There was the hostel...

Another of our mates had run to drop flat on his stomach in front of an excited group of our colleagues. Water! he coughed, Water! He rolled on his back. There came some faint excited . An eternity must have passed before he felt the blessed ɔlash all over his face. He turned on his belly. The water splashed on his head, ears and neck. He kicked and sprang to his feet.

That was Malik shaking his head and body like a cat shaking off water. Then I looked again and saw many others, haggard, bruised and fierce with excitement. Solidarity, they yelled. Solidarity, we chimed together.

Again came the sharp whistle of sirens loud and ominous. From the din someone shouted: "Look out!"

It was an incredible sight to behold. Tanks. Tanks were looming menacingly closer. "Those men are mad," a thin female voice screamed pointedly. "How dare they invade our quarters!"

But soon things were flying: Rat-tat-tat!

"Bullets!"

Terrified bodies surged to the wide panel-doorway, scrambling for a hold. Frantic screams were heard. I received a shove as if from an elephant and landed on the floor thoroughly jarred. Another followed. And then another.

But up again was I wading, treading through flesh and muscles. Once inside we ran up the stairs to the very last floor. From the safety of one of the hall rooms we stared and monitored the progress below. The tank had stopped some hundred yards away. Hooded figures, guns in their hands, prowled the ground, combat-ready. With quick furtive glances in every angle they brought down the barricades hastily tossed there by our gallant female comrades.

"Those bustards think they are fighting a war," I burst out spitefully.

"It's a war," another corrected.

Chin Ce

"Tanks against hands," I grimaced.

Hate burned in our eyes.

Several minutes later, with no visible life signs to shoot dead, the tank began to roll back. They beat a slow, reluctant retreat with wilder gun shots. Something landed near the power house and I saw the fumes rising steadily. There was going to be fire.

"They've put our power house on fire," Malik spat bitterly. The fire had turned to angry red flames and was spreading fast.

"We must put out that fire," someone ordered. We rushed down the stairs, down the dusty road not minding the sting of carbide. We poured sand and beat firmly. The fire was out minutes later. But we were not done yet.

"They have cordoned all routes into town," we discussed.

"But we must not be cowed. We will beat them to it..."

Our tactics were now cold and calculated.

"The rally must hold."

"Protest is our right."

"We must show that fat minister our placards," we agreed.

To penetrate the town meant to go in small, minor groups and meet in the stadium.

That was what we did. And it proved such a successful expedition into the stadium. Calmly we took positions in strategic corners near the soap box where the minister was billed to speak on Workers' Day.

It was a long wait for public officials who never kept to the hour. But we waited. The fool was two hours behind schedule. But there was no going back. We watched the short amorphous creature in May-day t-shirt. He lifted fat podgy hands to his forehead. Everyone rose to the dull loud clang of martial beats.

The more that raucous tune would play the more I analysed it. And the more I burned inside. What joker did that lyric in the first place? 'Compatriots' indeed. 'Fatherland?' Now what would you expect from a Nazi gang! I hissed disgustedly. 'Love?' Surely, gun totting thieves do not know love. It is brute power, not even strength. It is naked power that shoots and bombs its youth. 'Heroes,' I wanted to laugh. Those clowns were impossible. Heroes of greed and plunder. Perhaps in the far distant future there may be heroes, but certainly not the past and certainly not this present. Loud clang of cymbals... I saw the shapeless trunk of a hand drop limply down.

Now! We nudged each other. Now!

We leapt to the ground like a horde of bees, turning to face the government official.

"No to traitors!"our placards shouted high in the air.

"Who killed Dele Giwa?"

"Stop murdering the citizens!"

And from all corners of the stadium came a resounding wave of placards, clenched firsts. I smiled. This was the moment. I felt triumphant. The minister stood as if electrocuted; his jaws had dropped down the ground.

"Minister of Unemployment and Retrenchments!" a placard yelled at him.

We felt more triumphant, more powerful, than we ever did in our whole lives. This was sweet victory: the confusion of protest and violence.

Then from above the din came sirens... Crack shots rang through the air. Fumes rose thickly... squelching noises added to the din. Crack! And more crack! People lurched. Gasping, I barely caught hold of myself as I wobbled violently, my placard still gripped in my hand. There was blood... And panic. I dropped on one knee, quickly springing up in the confusion, and twisted and raced my way among the scattering confused bodies...

Then I was back again to the hall with a wakeful jerk.

Babul was now speaking in his kingly voice. "You see, you've been part of these movements all over the world; you swore to uphold the struggle forever, and now it's time to lead the pack," he frowned, raising a disapproving hand towards me, "you have begun to contemplate within yourself.

"But I say that is a wrong move, young man. You will soon find that people are better off with far less profundity. A single act of meditation sends many a loyal subject out on a foolish one man quest. Needless to say it only weakens your faith."

I had become quite uncomfortable there in the Mosque Hall. And Babul would not just shut up. I was annoyed with myself for letting him enter my past so easily and also allowing his rattling and whispering to get on my nerves.

Now the whole assembly, the speakers, hunched in their solemn dishonesty behind the long desk, and the interpreter ranting and making wild gestures with his fingers, were all very boring. The king's chatter worse, the disorganised voices and clamour outside the hall was worst.

"Do you see the fire of the mind?" Babul cried. "You have to learn, learn from the fire of the mind."

I decided it was time to leave. Why was I here anyway? I should leave Bill and Komas to have their fun. The roaring of the rouser might amuse the rabble. Afterall, they were all there to laugh and clap and sweep the solution into the tunnel. Even the dissent had quashed itself before it had even begun. This country was such a suffocating stereotype, like having to listen to a bad composition.

I rose to my feet and paced the passage spontaneously.

I felt strong disapproving eyes boring into me but I didn't mind them. I walked through the door and hovered uncertainly along the corridors where I paused to scan the electronic billboards where the pictures of the new leader of the nation were in full projection.

Komas and Billy appeared much later. They laughed in noisy whispers.

"Here he is, the traitor," Komas was winking rapidly in that absurd manner of his.

"Why did you leave like that man?" Billy demanded.

"How do you mean leave like that?" I was only too aware of

my sudden quiet disinterest.

"Abruptly! rudely! And with total disregard for decorum," Komas waved his arms. His face contorted with leering seemed, strangely enough, like Babul's.

"I thought I treaded as quietly as the mouse," I reminded them.

"You forgot we came together to join the others," Billy snapped, "I should have been watching the movie otherwise!"

"No. You would have been poking your life away at Games," I corrected. "Besides where is the Lady Protest now?" I asked.

But Komas changed the topic too soon.

"Man, you should have heard that brilliant expose on the likes of the interpreter."

"Who?" I asked, knowing I was there but wasn't really there.

"Tell him, Bill," Komas urged.

"I could barely hear a word of their raving," Bill replied. "Komas, that woman beside me, she was simply voluptuous, don't you think? I was ogling her all the time, practically raping her with my eyes…"

Bill waved him aside, and then painted the brilliant expose on the likes of Interpreter.Teacher had risen to the public challenge by the chief press secretary to the new government. He had called the interpreter a pawn of barbaric kings and queens, a fool in the game of medieval lords. The bearded fighter had nearly choked on his breath…

"Someone has said the truth about him at last," Komas went on, shaking his head in wonder and admiration.

Then it occurred to me, strange as it seemed, that if what Komas said was true, indeed, then one man had scored a bold victory against us all, speaking up for heaven and earth to hear.

Just one whistle blower in the whole of a million blind men.

To me, that meant Babul was not winning with the masses after all!

The Turning

*

Years back I would lie on my bed and watch my thoughts like wading flotsam across the screen of my mind. I was the seer: my tiny apartment was my memorial hall, the oracle that housed a particular chapter in the diary of my life. Once I entered it, the story opened to that same spot and the thoughts began to flow. A wild past I had mistaken for the present would spring to life to chatter their notes in my consciousness...

And behold it was I, a poor singer, indeed, who had repeated those jarring notes so tediously that the sheer inanity of the habit had brought Babul, the omnipresent sorcerer to my door...

But he would quickly disappear when I separated the flotsam of thoughts from my true self. The real *me* stayed knowingly calm while those shadow energies idled restlessly for a help in the form of attention to spring back to life and plague me with more and more of their energy sapping dramatics.

It was not until later that I realised, very subtly, that it was me who allowed the invasion of my mind by turning it into a magnet of sores which exacerbated the emotions and brought my life force on the spiral down the hopeless abyss where the bull cruised and would soon overtake my total initiative.

He always came again and again, like a phantom, that rampaging bull of terror who forced attention upon everything that upset the gaze -those time fragments which left the mind servile with guilt and thereby pliant to all kinds of suggestions.

And thus in my hall of memory was the song of all the flock

who were made to see their lot as poor, wretched and unworthy of saving grace -forever in need of a master and saviour.

In a way it would be incorrect to say this or that was how it started. Might just have been that this whole life and the lives before it were all programmed under the shadow of that huge spell. But 1984 had marked a turning point in my life. That year, a new convert had embraced a new life in the congregation of believers. A booming, commanding voice, which I later came to know belonged to the great bull, had spoken to me on the night of the frolic of Easter.

It was wierd in a funny way. I had rocked and rolled myself almost lame at a disco party the might before. I had sung and clapped with my friends till my voice was hoarse and my hands were sore. Finally I had drunk and gulped too much wine for my greedy pit of the belly. Now I was barely just alive, praying for the night to end my discomfort and the dawn to start a new day. It was in that sorry state, lying on the bed as I did now, and staring at the ceiling in that favourite posture of mine, but feeling terribly low down, that the voice stole in on me, reeling an old tune about the damnation which awaited me because of a sin into which my ancestors were born.

Incredible as the story was, I recalled the preacher had sermonised that previous day to the congregation that there was no escape from being damned and savaged in hell save in the blood of the lamb that had been killed but somehow got raised again that very day a few hundred years ago!

Thus was I uncharitably shown my wretchedness as in a black and white movie screen. To prove it all, the unpleasant details of my past misdeeds were added to memory. The result was guilt. A strange hypnotic guilt I never felt before, the kind that made all of us who fell in its grip ask that old question:

"Oh, what shall I do now?"

I had felt quite bad about my life and was determined to do something drastic about it. The voice ordered to abandon everything

I owned. I was to serve a term in the house of the lord until the moment came to be ordained his lifetime servant and holy minister.

Maloo, who was the lord's prophet, was to be my mentor.

Abandoning everything included my college love, Ima, too. Ah, that was the sad part, come to think of it now.

We would have made a nice couple and were looking forward to a promising future together. But now she was my salvation's major impediment in a very strange way.

Yet strange tall tales were easier to believe. I broke the sad news to her two weeks later after the short break as we sat under the cluster of some Pride of Barbados whose flowers had decorated the ground with dying red colours. The college was coming alive, ever so slowly, after the break. Now school, too, was all over for me. I never liked psychiatry anyway and always had that feeling it was not the job of people nearly sick in the head to nurse other people who were also sick in the head.

Knees hunched close, a light wind laced its feathery hands across my temple, caressing me. The twilight was coming out of a golden slumber to shower its colour over the little college campus. It was a painful moment for us but the zeal of a new convert was deadly serious and surpassed all reason. The lord had spoken, I told her, expecting her to understand. But Ima sat stock still and stared incredulously. "Why would God tell you to abandon dear ones simply to serve him?"

I shook my head sympathetically. Ima did not understand the ways of the lord.

"The old ways must disappear to make for a completely new life," I tried to explain, patiently, watching her snort in derision.

"What goes of the old?"

I was puzzled by her question.

"I mean the old ways," she teased. "What goes?"

I was silent.

"This is only your mind playing tricks on you," she fired point blank, and that truly hurt.

Our meeting had ended sooner than intended and we had parted ways.

I took on my training with zeal -a one-track eagerly self centred zeal. Nothing else could matter.

I broke off communication with friends on the outside world in order to concentrate fully and without distraction on my new role within the fellowship. Behind this was the secret ambition to beat them to the crowning glory on the final day. Bill, Komas and others would still be taking school lessons by the time I would have become an anointed minister.

My early duty as a steward of the holy lord after the prophet consisted of leading the prayer wing of the new members. My dancing and singing had found better use. In a short time I had waxed two beautiful albums of music the lyrics gently pirated from early seventies Rock'n'Roll and Rhythm'n'Blues. Of course, the flock didn't know this part. I dedicated all to the holy prophet and sponsor of my work. That was rare privilege for the fame it brought. The women who with children formed the bulk of the following admired and sent gifts. Some of those I modestly accepted as part of the gains of the calling.

It wasn't long before the younger ones began to make private visits for counselling. Sometimes these began to prolong into the night and ended in lots of crying and hugging. I noticed these flip sides always took place when Maloo would be out on late night visitations.

More startling requests increased with my growing stature in the ministry as Maloo's possible successor. Decisively I turned down several other requests for holy bath, holy massage, et cetera from barren women and young married ones looking to have children. So what if the prophet was doing it? Their overtures puzzled me. Their practised ease at it repelled me. I began to avoid close contacts and turned down personal home invitations with great courtesy. It was difficult to imagine the pressure that men of God faced with their flock. Everyone seemed to look up to my handsome features for the proof of my mission. To the young women of the ministry it was a sort of pride to be in public and private company with their gifted dramatist of song, dance and prayer.

Under a few months I made a dizzying ascension through the ranks. However, from the beginning through the course of my time handling the sermon from the mighty pulpit, I was willing to let my roles be groomed by my conscience and inner revelation. I stood firm against any stories of violence in the teachings which were often the cause of serious misgivings in my mind. I had considered the bloodiness of religious history and saw myself as the emergent inheritor of a glorious promise to reform both self and mission in humble submission to peace and happiness.

Like the prophets I was here to do and say as God had directed me. I would heal the sick and make barren wombs bear fruits again, not literally but by the power of my song and the faith of my vision. Finally I would come into the glory of these mighty works only as the servant of my heavenly father. What else could I want? Here was the power to bring souls netted from the river of life at the feet of the lord. That other power that evoked fear and awe, the power of the bull among the flock, I had observed closely, must be tempered for the love that bound all men, women and of course animals and plants, every living and non living thing, in one universal brotherhood of peaceful and loving ascension. There was to be no preachment about the fiery brimstone in the great beyond where any feet who treaded never returned. Love, not fear, was to be the bond that glued the flock together and made the conscience central to salvation from bondage to material existence.

In the dying days of the twelfth month, close to the completion of my work, doubts began to set in as to my success with my mission as I believed it to have been revealed to me. Something within me gnawed deeply; it brought back a distant flicker of Ima's inner presence, a sour reminder of our last blunt farewell and the happiness that was now missing inside me. In spite of my success and popularity rating in the ministry, I was a lonely and sad man at heart and something was telling me these were not the true signs of being in the lord.

But it was the fate of a middle aged widow and her only daughter which crystallised my lingering doubt into an instant revelation and I began to call for the immediate release of souls in bondage by the feet of the very prophet and man of God that was supposed to liberate them.

One night after I had switched out the lights of the central mission parlour which served as the prophet's visitor's room and was preparing to say my prayers for the night there came a loud banging on the door.

I hesitated. I was afraid, and this surprised me. I wondered if it was the prophet himself who was out on his weekend visitations. But it was unlikely to be Maloo. His holy visits were wont to last till nearly daybreak and it was only midnight by the wall clock donated by women elders. Shouldn't the man of God rather be ministering to some barren women in their houses now? Gingerly I peeped through a parted window blind. It was dark outside but the hundred watt bulb over the door provided some light. It illuminated the face of my surprise visitor, a deeply peaceful yellow glow on a pale skin. She wore only a short dark blouse and a single wrapper tied loosely around her waist. Her hair which appeared to have been permed a long time now hung carelessly over her shoulders giving her a wild look. I recognised ma Tandi the widow with an only daughter, a close family friend of the prophet, and so moved urgently to unlatch the door.

She came in with mad urgency and wild manners asking, no, shouting to see the dog of the house who would have her daughter's womb for his ritual.

I recalled vividly my shock at her language, and to my question as to what was wrong, her daughter was dying, she screamed. "Tell the bastard to come and undo what he's done to her -or else..." her voice rattled loudly in the dead of the night.

To say I was embarrassed would be an awful understatement. She had already stomped off as dramatically as she arrived banging the door with a shattering impact. "And if anything happens to her," ma Tandi's words echoed in my ears like the ominous drumming of the night masquerade.

The great spokesman of the lord received the news with a violent oath, then quickly comported himself before me and promised to fix the matter straight away. Only a minor problem, he promised and then with a hastiness that belied his dignified composure he grabbed the door and was out in the darkness, his gown blending rapidly in the gathering dawn.

Maloo must have fixed the matter too well, for on Sunday, which was the next day, from the top of the rostrum, he confirmed the astonishing transition of Zahara, ma Tandi's only daughter. The poor widow had finally lost her mind from the shock of her disaster and could not even remember her surroundings or who she was. She would be confined to the inner sanctuary where some women devotees will pray for her, he told all of us. The flock gaped and clasped their arms speechless. A familiar terror filled the hall while prophet Maloo, messenger of the lord, gave a sermon on salvation and the theme was Hell as a real place for sinners.

The flock never knew what killed Zahara, only the young man, as I was being called during my rebellion, had a vague idea. As usual, there were so many things happening in the holy sanctuaries that the masses in their herds would never know. For me, the man who knew just a little, the successive nights were to become a terrifying nightmare as I battled with myself.

I was afraid of the knowledge that Maloo had the life of his members in his hands in some cruel, secret manner. It disturbed me, upset my meditative tranquillity. Then it made me lose some regard for these men and the teaching they represented so efficiently and callously.

My dissent began to show when I bluntly refused to lead the prayer wing in singing and dancing performance. That had become a stereotype which made me feel like a clown, a fool, dancing from the light into darkness while the demons wearing the visage of angels twiddled us in their fingers. I countered all requests to remember the sick woman in daily prayers and demanded instead that a licensed physician be allowed to see ma Tandi and determine her true state of mind.

It was the vision of a woman abused that gave me a bad conscience and made me wish to be no further part of Maloo's story. If ma Tandi was alive then we should set her free. I called for her release every night and day. What claim had any one over the freedom of another in the name of God? By the time it was finally announced that ma Tandi too had passed away in grief, the nobility of priesthood had crumbled before me like a pack of cards. And I realised that I had virtually quit well ahead of my induction within that grand circular game of blind belief and worship.

It took great courage to admit to myself that there was something that rang false in the doctrine of Maloo's God. And to be perpetrator or victim in the play appealed to me no more. Both choices would have me in a spiral. For what was self annihilation but the denial of peace to souls who yearned for it? And what was evil but the transformation of higher purpose to selfish ends. To manipulate the lives and deaths of others was so heinous that it made Maloo and the lord he served the worst con artists in human history.

I still recalled my decision after that moment of revelation to disavow the path I had chosen that night of my own Easter resurrection. I wanted my resignation to be public and final -to stir the mind of people to think for themselves- on that day of ordainment.

But it never occurred to me that Babul, the lord of the story, would himself swing an incredible power against me.

Nagua's Gift

*

Coming to think of it now, I could still have been the victim of an insidious programme of dominion if I had not met Nagua and held his rescue gift in my palms.

Nagua's gift was a large loose bound note. "The gift of memory," he had told us -just before we parted. "Inside can be found everything you have forgotten. And you can only so seek as to begin to remember again."

The first letters had stared at me with the words: "All things become clear when we return to the beginning of it all in the great continuum of being." Those were strange words that I had never read before in any story book. And inside was late ma Tandi looking resplendent and full of life. Ma Tandi killed by Babul's mayor. She had on a silk cotton dress that covered her neck; her eyes were bright as were her lips from which flowed strangely familiar phrases that were barely audible.

I flipped the pages for the stories to come alive. Each page unlocked a memory that expanded my mind and lighted my quest beyond all I had ever imagined before now. Presently there leapt upon me a section that told itself in the voice of the widow woman. It said: "Unknown to me, I was searching for something that was not there among the legions of Babul, something which no one could ever give me because it belonged to me by right.

"Then my being was not wholly immersed in the spirit of all life, to move, act with true knowledge and responsibilty for self.

"So I could never rise to claim it, having not jettisoned the last pang of fear to see through the threat of the monster and expose the futility of his power.

"And so you must know, dear friend, that the choice to leave our mother Earth was mine and mine alone.

"For no one had the power to destroy us or any other soul for that matter; to distract us, yes, this was done to me, to invade our minds, render us unable to remember, yes, for just a little while.

"But to annihilate your being would be the most sham and bogus claim in the book of letters. The bull was still a blind and limited force that fed on the ignorance and cowardice of the herd..."

I flipped randomly until coming to the end and closed the book in my hands. Then I heaved a deep sigh. Here was the great story; the rousing of one among, and for, the many. The gratefulness of knowledge seemed now an intrinsic part of my thinking. For the first time I felt truly alive. It had taken just that moment to come into this awakening. Never again was I going to accept any delusion on the fringe of my mind. From now on my head would be mine to carry and protect from the beast and his hooded agents. Never would the tragedy of the frightful fall upon me again...

Immediately there came a flash, a light of cognition, and then a sound of thunder. Something had happened. The scales had fallen from my eyes. A great relief had settled over me.

With that simple change of attitude an overwhelming discovery of beauty was breaking upon the universe. I discovered that through all my delusions, my intentions had been genuinely selfless nevertheless, borne from a sincerity that helped to usher the new reality I was to create from now on. And with these thoughts in mind, I drifted into a state of restfulness and peace for perhaps the first time in many years.

But it does seem like I'm telling it all in reverse mode, doesn't it? Now, to how I met Nagua...

It was in a dream world where everything seemed to change; for once there was no monster masquerade, no bull chase and the nightmare battles. It was a girl whose fragrance like a flower once lit all the centres within me. Ima was a familiar angel with whom I had parted ways for some time in not too happy circumstances. Who would have thought I could come back to her again. My heart thumped. A serenade sang in my heart. I wanted to speak beautiful words to her this time and not the selfish abandonment of the past, but I couldn't get them together. My apologia tumbled jerkily from my mouth.

"Why have you returned?" Ima asked.

Strangely she was almost without emotion. There was neither pride nor indignation in her voice, just a question which both of us knew the answer. We sat side by side on a brown footstone under a low pine tree which whistled softly and endlessly.

It was a dreamy world. The sun was a pink, soft glow that blended gently with the soft bluish hue of the clouds that drifted so low overhead that we should reach out and feel them in our hands. So close was everything, like the wind that rustled the pine. I could reach out to all things in this world by simply thinking of their beauty. There was an intimacy in both of us that filled all space. I seemed to know many things yet there were so many things I was still to learn.

"I wronged you, Ima," I finally began. "I came to say sorry for leaving the way I did. That was hardly the way to treat a friend."

Yet in spite of the peace and harmony around me the words stuck in my throat. I felt like a prodigal. But Ima brushed this aside with the words: "No need for that," and a wave of her hand. She reached out to prod the soft soil, scooping a handful of brown, yellow sand to let them sift gently though her parted fingers. "We cannot be sorry for the past; it's useless in the moment the answers are found," she said.

"I'm not clinging at all in the past," I countered. "But better to correct them in order to move on with our lives..."

Her laughter rang out in the clear lustre of the pink sunshine. "There's nothing to correct when all is well. You always think in terms of wrong. But all is right here and now that brings us joy and beauty."

I looked at her wonderingly. This was a new girl in a short period. She looked more sanguine than I had known her to be. Her youth and beauty shone with confidence and careless disinterestedness which seemed to underline her confidence and strength. It was like the strength of a panther.

She must have caught my thoughts and was rather bemused. "You see, you left for your mission and then I found the oracle. Nagua."

"Nagua," I repeated. "Who is Nagua?"

Then it dawned on me. Ima had a new man in her life. A surge of emotion shot through me. I thought I was back with the girl of my dream and she was talking about another with such daintiness, and delight. But Ima laughed, throwing away sand from her hands and rising simultaneously to her feet. "Isn't it beautiful" she exclaimed, "the loneliness of the world and the companionship of your soul."

The wind was blowing higher: some invisible beings that could only be felt and heard as sound. So was the rustling of the lone pine tree. It was a silent land spread-eagled like an endless beautiful wild, and coloured with the unreality of pink majestic energy through the still overhead sky. "Come let's play," she called to me and without looking back, bounded gracefully into the wild brush.

I watched her for a few seconds, envying the joy and freedom of her every movement, the nimbleness of her body and the ease with which she glided in the air, hands spread out, beautiful round legs slightly poised for balance and then it struck me how evenly balanced she was in her world. The more I watched her, the more it stirred in me an inner vigour, the strength to move, to forgo everything past and move into the fullness of living expression.

"Come," Ima's voice from the distance wafted close. I rose to my feet, unsure of my steps, trying to find my balance as my left leg caught in the sand and my right slipped and my hands flailed briefly, a novice at the balancing act.

Then letting go my attention on myself to concentrate on the élan from in the distance, I was soon sailing effortlessly, cutting through the moaning wind spirits whose sound had heightened to a great reverberating drone. I sped and the sun's brilliance spread out to me her warm embrace in freedom and joy. Suddenly I felt myself in the soft pliant arms of my friend. Ima giggled into my face. A halo was spreading over her head. "How do you feel now?" she shouted in the noise of the irrepressible wind.

"I feel I can do anything I need. You feel it too?"

She laughed in answer.

"And do I have that light on my head?" I pointed. I was joyous and excited at the experience I was having in this beautiful corner of the universe.

"If you can see it then there it is," she teased.

And sure enough I could feel a dancing and glowing around my face and head and cheeks, and all over my body. It was all around me like a huge globe. I stretched my hands and beams of light flashed out like lightning colours of white, blue and yellow. Ima joined and soon we were throwing many colours of light crisscrossing like fireworks. I threw a dart at her which she deftly deflected with a bright beam. "Defend yourself," she declared as we threw and parried darts. "I am Sepa of the golden flame. And what are you called?"

I paused and her beam caught me on the shoulder knocking me flat to the ground. I reeled in pain. Ima laughed.

"It's only your mind," she told me. "Nothing really hurts you in this sphere."

Then I stopped, transfixed by the most incredible vision I ever saw. The beings of the universe!

There they were hovering above, around, within and without. They were strangely familiar faces. I recognised them all: fathers, mothers, grandfathers and stepmothers, aunts and uncles, great uncles and a host of friends and relations I never recalled existed before. I saw the ancients of days in the entire universe from across all races of the known and unknown cosmos. These were my ancestors, our higher companions who watched over us, silently, quietly always there in the background of all things, all events, guiding, nurturing and ever so gently, bringing us closer into the fuller realisation of our purpose in this world. These were my universal family! And they were calling my name in the softest, gentlest notes of music I ever heard. "Kusun!" I announced with great delight, leaping like a teen who had only just found the solution to a life long puzzle. "I am Kusunku; I am the son of the bright morning sun!"

The proclamation was like a healing trumpet, the last blast in the awakening of a mind. I was like one for whom a bad spell had been broken and could see clearly now, for the first time in a long, long while. I sat down to savour this silent thrill of recovery. Ima drew closer, placing a gentle hand around my neck. "How great to welcome you back, flame of my heart!"

I smiled as she stretched her hand to me. I took it and she pulled me up my feet. "Come let's wait. The search is nearly over. "For Nagua."

The dull ache of sorrow returned. We were back again under the pine tree, sitting side by side, knees drawn up, our hands clasped over the knees. After a very long time had passed with Ima searching the distance with squinted eyes, I asked again. "Who is Nagua?"

Ima narrowed a pair of bright, intelligent eyes that were scanning the horizon, as if expecting something to turn up there that very moment. "You know, there are times," she said, "that you sound as if I will understand you full well only when we return to that great continuum of being."

"Why is that?" I asked sheepishly.

"You act all from the mind without," her eyes flashed a sudden brilliant light. "When will you trust in your deepest heart within?"

I looked into her eyes; her radiant white gleamed softly, tenderly. The twinkle had not gone; it was there, faintly though, drenched in a softness which bore compassion flowing like a spring. I clasped my arms around her neck, melting completely in her warmth and trust.

Presently she exclaimed. "There's Nagua! He's coming our way." And she was off in a quick sprint.

I followed her beautiful legs flitting nimbly across the rich ochre coloured soil toward a shadowy outline. As we drew close I saw the figure looked strangely familiar in his bright white top and dark hued trousers. And when he turned to meet us I realised with a jolt of surprise how foolish I had been to entertain doubts about the girl.

Nagua was the courageous old teacher I had admired at the auditorium of national conference. And the old teacher grinning wolfishly at us was no other than the greatest story teller that ever lived in the Kongo tribe of Omaha and the whole country of Naigon: Onku himself!

The Return

*

I roused alert later that evening trying to fully remember. In my thought, Ima hovered gently and firmly. I had not forgotten the old teacher and the dialogue we had, and I was to remember later that evening everything we had said and agreed that I must do next to fulfil the purpose of this story.

Now it was Ima's presence I felt everywhere. It was a calming, loving presence and I looked forward to meeting her soon. Her companionship had always been there, beyond words and my mind's interpretation. Her eyes that flashed with feline beauty had more promise than the allure of all of Babul's women who would only drag one down and deep into a point of no return in worship of a lord and master of their fates.

Here I was lord of the self. My mission was what needed be done at every given moment. Ima was a member of my higher companions, and one that I had only just discovered. The prodigal had come back never again to live among the swine and dirt of ignorance. At last, the son of the sun of the universe had found a way.

Murder

*

I t was a day to the ordainment. News of it was everywhere in the papers, on radio and television. Pictures of Baba, patron of the saints, filled the pages and screens. The entire priesthood was in a frenzy. Everything must be ready for the coming of the lord and master of heaven to consecrate the holy initiation of his new ministers and priests. No member of the salvation should be caught napping on that day even if it meant the Baptist walking from house to house to prepare the way and wake up the sleeping. That was Maloo's job, I guessed, as he pushed open and bashed into my mental chamber that morning.

"How now," he grinned evilly, "how's the rebel making out?"

I appraised the invader who pretended to be my guide and liked to be called man of God after his forebears from the barren land of Judah. I regarded the familiar tunic he wore around his neck so perpetually it was obvious he slept in it. It was the only semblance of brightness around him, a thin mud white band. All else from head to toe was the black hood that was the trademark of his calling.

"By the way, I am now His Most Reverend Mayor Maloo - Special Deputy of our Father by His Grace," he introduced garrulously. "Well, the great Bull will be presenting me publicly to the congregation," he winked proudly.

"What do you want?" I asked him, my tone neither hostile nor too particularly friendly. The lord had been called by every name from the animal world to the mineral kingdom as far as I could remember. It mattered no longer from whose lips every blasphemy proceeded against the deity.

Maloo looked startled, or pretended to be. "I will be working again with you as your Father Superior, don't forget. The favourite chicks are not allowed to wander far from the mother hen," he pacified a proverb, pulling a seat closer and sitting down his backside gingerly. "How did you like my talk at the confere asked patronisingly.

"I was late," I replied. "It was the interpreter who had the day."

"Not so fast," the reverend mayor countered, "*I* had the day. I led the opening and closing prayers to the almighty Father. At those moments, I was the most important personage in the whole nation. All the tribes and their rulers, wherever they were, said 'Amen' to my prayers and invocations."

"I can imagine," I sneered, "how you thoroughly enjoy that sordid world of prostitution."

Mayor shrugged. "If you must put it so uncharitably, religions are mere prostitutes in the form of institutions," he conceded, but on a grudging note added, "so is everything else."

"What of the interpreter?" he continued. "He is a scribbler, remember? And they are the worst of prostitutes, scuttling after dictators with their writing papers. My God, have they debased the sacredness of writing! That's why we keep them off scripture," muttered the man of God in his righteous sense of indignation.

"Scripture," I gave a short derisive laughter. "The one you wrote?"

"Well, the flock is not complaining," the preacher countered, shrugging his dark hooded shoulders. "You don't blame us when we say scripture was written with the finger of God. Otherwise, I tell you, we won't have one member of the fold remaining. Tell them God is at the north pole of the equator and you have them in their hundreds nodding in that direction. It tames their animal natures. But say God is everywhere and... well," he shrugged again, "we'd sooner have dissenters like you who'd start to think us hardly relevant in this world anymore."

"They should be told the truth, and you must honour the

freedom of choice in Creator's universes," I retorted.

"But we've not come to that stage of human development yet," he countered furiously. "Neither truth nor freedom but massive loyalty and grouping, that's the business we're here for," Mayor insisted.

"You take away our right like you tether a herd," I was hating this man now more than ever.

The Prophet threw up his hands angrily. "We take our doctrine from His Holiness, the Father. You are not His Holiness!

"And I tell you," he reminded me, "the Conquering Lion is still a rampaging Bull even now. And he has the whole world in his hands forever." Throwing a conspiratorial glance, he continued the robotic repetition of sham and doctrine. "So you may know this, we are one body in a mass... and these sects you find here and there are all sons of the same old man. Many years ago, he told me, rousers like you made so much noise that he commissioned another son to constitute the commie doctrine to preach the might of the masses...

"That tamed the craze for some time. Now you are here talking about truth, freedom, which is impossible to define... Baba will not let this happen; otherwise we will have all converts fleeing into the green fields. That kind of thing upsets business, you know... It happened before and we wiped them off the four corners with the Inquisitions.

"Where do you think we will be with all these talk about truth and freedom?" The prophet was getting worked up now, but he managed to calm down after a while and was soon giving me his deceptively broad smile. "You see, what took you so long to come into the service of the Lord is this unending dissent..."

"I like to think I've come a long way," I interrupted -the same reply I gave waB when he led the hounds after me. The circle had come full round again and the same prospect now faced me. What was I to do next? The preacher's smile turned a grimace.

"You keep saying those words every time. That was how you stormed out of the ceremony, your own induction. You were an embarrassment to everyone.

"Imagine how our great father presented himself that day. He did not send a representative, mind you but... he manifested his very presence, like he will do tomorrow, to consecrate your induction himself," Mayor shook his head sadly.

"But you stormed away, embarrassing us before the lord. That was when everything turned personal, became an ego thing, you know. Let me tell you, Baba was very angry. And waB and the hounds went after you. It was the worst example to set before the congregation...just the way you walked out of the conference yesterday. You don't assert your dissent against a powerful body like that, but that is what you do, you and that stupid story teller they call teacher."

"Teacher is a visionary, truer to his mission than all of us put together -all of us who kept sealed lips about your murders and deceit for years," I said.

"A sealed lip is better for you," the prophet uttered callously. "This teacher, he makes trouble for us with his whistle tales. He speaks a load of rubbish and angers the faith a lot. We may have to take him out over time, as we did to other dreamers who claimed to be sons of God too. O, Blasphemy," he blocked his ears with his fingers exactly in the manner of Babul.

"You take out only the body and not the soul, what use? Zahara and her mother, they live. Their ideas live in the seeds of the earth; they grow, bloom and add more force to the gathering of enlightened souls."

"That too we don't preach," Mayor Maloo insisted. "The soul that sinneth shall die. That is what we teach... But let's not go into scripture now. Young man, you must stop all this rebellion if you must grow in the fold." Maloo was the ape of Babul and his mannerisms. Between both I could not tell who detested me more. That's the problem with brainwashing, I was thinking to myself. The flock aped the priests, the priests aped their high lords, and before you knew it, every member you met was an ape of some other in the hierarchy, and you could trace the same talk and act way back to their great lord and master -Babul.

"You have a strong spirit, father has told me, great power of leadership and the lord has called you to net in the fishes in the sea. What more could you want? I tell you, the reward in cash and kind..." Mayor shook his head. "It's a mistake to quit the flock. I came to warn you. Never do that again. You invite the Inquisition on your head.

"Luckily there's atonement for heretics today. We may not burn them at the stake anymore. Secular laws have scored a cheap point there," he acceded as an afterthought, folding his black garments in his laps and adjusting his seat. "But remember," he glowered at me with a dangerous gleam in his eyes, "we still pass the death bill underhand. The teacher shall have it tomorrow." The last threat was a whisper that was meant for me as well as his supposed victim, Nagua.

I replied that I was not too shocked that the lone, undaunted voice telling it to them exactly as it was, without fear or favour, would be marked for elimination by the cabal that controlled the mind of the masses through the CPS and himself reverend Maloo. Nagua's voice would still talk without fear even if his head were severed from his body, I told him.

"A talking head?" Mayor sneered. "We shall see then." His tone was final. His plan was made.

Then I recalled the great eagle's appearance to me and Ima the very first time in that land of the golden sun and ochre rich soil...

We had hugged and greeted each other. I was full of respect for the good fellow and I felt the teacher held us in equal high esteem too. I had mentioned his brave utterances at the conference, but he had brushed it aside as really of little significance. It was a ploy, he said, to control the awakening among the people. The interpreter and his network -pawns of the darkness- had sworn to glorify every fool from the military barracks and civilian gutters. The plan was to make lap dogs of the people -weak ones like themselves, tethered to their gifts and licking power boots on radio waves and news pages. Then Nagua said: "Never forget you are Kusunku of the Eagle clan; your voice and deed must carry far and boldly into the very recesses of the world's heartbeat, so that a few that are ready will hear and awaken..."

I recalled those very words now as clearly as it was in the realm of vision.

And presently looking at Prophet Mayor as he talked, I felt a beastly urge to grab him by the neck and tear him to pieces. This was the man who murdered Zahara and her mother after having used and abused them both in his church. This was the most insensitive pawn of the evil creature that men worshipped for power and dominion over their fellows. Yet, alone, he was only a vegetable, an empty fleshly vessel that dreaded his mortality as fervently as he impressed it upon the ignorant and exploited the weak in his fold.

Oblivious of his danger, the mayor was still speaking, or rather blowing his fumes of vengeance and wrath. "There must be a limit for those know-alls in this country. I'll call the secret elite to meet and decree that teacher must be assisted to an early exit from this world. I'll sponsor the bill," he smacked his lips; his eyes gleamed evilly. "How could anyone insult God in public glare, calling all of us a monstrous manipulation to bind the world in fear and ignorance? He scored a cheap victory there and the youth dispersed more heretical than before, making nonsense of the whole process. For that, he must pay with his life. And you must learn and beware."

I sprang at him with a sudden wild hiss; my fingers became barred talons of the eagle race of my clan. So sudden and unexpected was my action that the prophet was sitting duck. My weight crashed down on him. My hands found his neck and gripped like a vice. The prophet's startled cry was promptly muffled. Gurgling for breath and lashing out with frenzied fists, Mayor thawed and clawed. I held my breath, empowered by wild vicious rage. Maloo's eyes rounded in terror. He must have realised he was going to die suffocating in my hands and he managed a short gurgle of panic. But his strength failed him rapidly, strength dissipated by years of soft, wasting indulgence on the crooked labours of his followers. I had my iron weight on his chest as I throttled the life out of him. Anger had overpowered my mind. Pushed beyond its limit, only hatred and revulsion for the dark form that sprawled and thrashed under my weight filled my heart.

I did not stop until I had snuffed his breath and heard his ghost shrieking wildly into the yawning abyss of darkness and terror that waited for him in the nether world. Then my grip slackened and quick as a falcon, I sprang. I was up on my feet and leaning against the wall, panting just a little to regain my breath.

For several minutes or thereabout I was motionless, trying to think more clearly. It surprised me how sudden rage had snapped the hair's thread to a killing. Mere seconds of revolt had brought me down the headlong route with the likes of the man who revolted me.

Not that I had any regrets for what I had done. I watched from an angle of my eyes the sprawled lifeless body among broken wood, a ghastly bruise by the side of his neck. His black garment, crumpled, hung ungracefully from his frame like a useless sack.

Thus lay Reverend Father Mayor, the coward who, even at his old age, had been terrified of the death he decreed and inflicted upon others so mindlessly. He was never to invade my mind again. It was a threat that had ended. Ended too was the power to control the minds of his flock and bring them to harm at will. And as Nagua had told us in the land of the golden sun, whoever showed strength against the minions of Babul on earth was surely the Father Superior of his world anywhere in the universe of myriad lives.

And so it was that I finally did summon enough courage to keep my head in the face of a great trick that nearly fooled my mind. The last step now was to confront the evil master himself face to face at his own demesne in the discarnate realm.

Confrontation

*

Crossing the borderline of the earth and into the fringe of the nether world was like delving in a moving screen where ugly shapes and dull colours were thrown before the vision in random, fuzzy black and white. The weird gurgling and howling of captive souls assailed your hearing, and the dizzying flight of life forms added to the horrendous illusion while you steadied your balance on the narrow path. One step out of turn was all it took to fall back into a warring world where you would battle to break free from the tyranny of materialism and confusion.

And so with care and courage, I treaded. That was the sure way, Nagua told me, to trace Babul, the acclaimed lord, to his lair. I had to confront him for the last time with the secret he had hidden from his human slaves for so long.

Because no longer was I his quarry. I had stepped past the fear and indecision that paralysed the minds of Earth children for many, many generations.

A spiral of white smoke from the conclave made it easy to locate the chimney tower of Babul's residence. There he fed from the energy of the billions he had won to himself in worship and devotion.

The approach was strangely unguarded save for few shadow energies that took form every now and then and tried to dig into your fears and grab at your mind. Babul knew none of his earth loyalists could summon the courage to journey out of their bodies, past the tunnel of terror, and the valley of the shadow of death, to venture here.

None, save a few priests of his cabal.

Well, I was neither his follower nor his priest in the strictest terms. For some time now, I had only been his fodder, but unlike most, an unwilling one. Now the matter had complicated further. The weaver of illusions who swallowed the tale of his own omnipotence in the literal sense of every bad fable had proven complacent to credit anyone else with some intelligence. He had become the tortoise who thought he had all the wisdom of the world inside his personal calabash. Well, a surprise now awaited him.

I edged my way gingerly, ignoring the hazardous motions around me.

Babul's minions!

They were prancing in and out and poking mischief on my vision. Formless and lurid, manifested by vile thoughts, they sought outlets in the depressing miasma of any mind open to them.

It was there that his power lurked, digging his forays onto souls, and manifesting as fast as their pitiful thoughts of their own unworthiness attracted him. I waved aside a green faced one brandishing a weapon in my face. It fell back into the shadows with a puff!

The thick grey cloud of mist around the hearth soon became a circle of dull red walls at whose tin-clad entrance stood waB the daemon. Beside this loyal servant at the gate was a green faced animal sentry who seemed impervious to the lewdness around her with waB massaging her fleshed out derriere while she gave excited grunts and an empty look in space.

Then my eyes met waB's.

The hound leader was wearing his beastly hooded visage and a red band around his snout. He was genial this time in his greeting. "There you are," he greeted, his hand dropping lazily to his side. "I was watching out for you, just in case."

This last one was a lie. In a way he was saying it was known that I would be coming here at that very moment, and he was just there to receive me. waB had grown adept at the art of dissembling that went with the craft. It kept the audience in awe that the priest, like his God, knew everything that could happen at any crucial moment in the lives of his devotees. But that was the ruse of the text.

Deftly he motioned the animal woman to hold on. She was now sheep staring at me with naked desire and chewing frantically on what must be flesh gums in her mouth.

"Follow me," he turned, leading the way, still not resisting the urge to lay his hands around that derriere in a parting gesture.

Then he hobbled forward, a silhouette in the twilight. His dirty whiskers bristled in the grey smoke. His eyes darted left and right. He made a noise as if to throw up sputum or something else. Finally, he seemed to think otherwise and gave a short uneasy laugh.

"That day of the chase was nothing personal; just orders," he began. "Surely, as one of us, you must understand."

I gave him silence as we clumped through an ancient dilapidated hallway covered with dirty slivery soot and webs. Everything here seemed fallen despite the stockpile of smoke and mirrors that threw multiple images all over the corners.

"Man, I am so relieved you're back with us. I can't tell you how scandalising it is to fight a fellow brother in the cause. Anyhow," he sounded a trifle apologetic, "with permanent interests in focus, the enemy today may be the friend tomorrow."

"That open secret," I replied indifferently, "Isn't it the cornerstone of all lies?"

waB gave a short, uneasy laugh.

"You have a strange sense of humour, man. There's nothing we have that you seem to care for. Even the dos don't seem to hold water with you. Let alone the don'ts"

"As if they ever watered anyone's garden in the beginning," I snorted.

"They work, and they do not work. I want and then I do not want. That's what beats me well under the heat," waB broke off.

"You get what I mean?"

I shook my head. "Not any more, when you see the trick of the tale, you are bound to a wake up call."

"Trick of the tale," he gave a smirk. "I can see why everyone told Baba you could be the ruin of us. Your ideas will do away with the only story we cherish so much; now that's close to heresy. A tale may be a tale but we need loyal bearers for them ...um um", he cleared his throat in a conciliatory tone. "All you see here is... personal, you know. We can't be too discreet about our affairs. Was that not the ruin of Pastor and Mayor?" he sounded strangely rhetorical."

"Or the beginning of their ruin," I smiled to him. "Don't worry, you are none of my business, you never were," I assured him. "After all, you are my kinsman, waB"

He grinned back, not understanding my meaning but blurting in his mechanical manner. "Who knows, one day, we could even become first cousins by his lordship... Now here is His Holiness," said the priest daemon, bowing very low.

He sat on a high stool decked with red and glittering sliver stones. The blood-red hood covered from his huge beastly shoulders to his toes. You could imagine a primeval lord hunched in a high seat, the giant mirrors adding to his imposing size as he glowered down to his subjects below.

Babul was flanked by over a hundred high priests of his inner sanctum. They were dressed in the ceremonial garb of crimson hoods, holding dim lighted objects in each hand which caught the mirrors and threw gleams around a dome that slanted dangerously above. The beast gave a satisfied nod to his priest and almost began to sniff the air around me.

"You come to me with courage. But I see vexation in your aura," he began.

I smiled at him.

"Congratulations, young man, you have made it. Are you not

honoured to be counted among the high priests of the realm? This is a great occasion in your life."

"Great indeed," I interrupted, aware of the frown of disapproval from his hood as I walked straight up the raised dais on which he sat. It happened in seconds, too quick for Babul's expectation. It brought sharp muffled gasps of surprise from the congregation.

"Now get your minions out of sight. I want to speak to you alone," I began in a quick, calm and determined voice. "In your own interest, Babul," I added, "for you won't like them to hear what I have to say, I assure you."

His Holiness was taken aback. But one look into my eyes decided for him. He waved a left to his men and, in a minute, the rigid, immobile order of psychic moguls disappeared through hidden doors in the wall. I glanced around a few seconds to be sure. Even the daemon waB was nowhere to be seen.

"Good," I began, "I have come to see you Babul, I guess you know by now I will neither serve nor be herdsman of your force in any way."

"You gave your silent agreement to that duty," Babul snarled. He was clearly exasperated with what was becoming my eternal merry go round with him on the subject of tending more slaves on earth. "When you put your hands on my plough, there's no going back!" his voice became a bellow that resounded with loud echoes in the open debris of his kingdom.

But I was unperturbed. His game was winding full circle in his face. You have to get used to the two faces of this lord of hosts. The benign face he reserved to loyal worshippers under his influence; the demonic visage he welded against any who dared doubt on some matters of contradiction in his cock and bull tales. At this point I couldn't give a whiff for either.

"It's not my fault how you interpret silence. Listen," I stared into his mean, indulgent snout, "and I will tell you my tale..."

"Oh ho, you own the tale now," Babul laughed in derision but he was uneasy as far as I could sense the air around him.

The Oracle

"What you don't know is a tale that must be told, my friend."

"Oh ho, I'm now your friend," Babul scorned again. "You never called me that before, did you?" his face puckered with rage. "I am your lord!" he made that reverberating bellow again.

"You forgot to add 'master,' I calmly retorted. "Not that it matters any longer. Now listen to my story. A long, long time ago, there were two brothers. And there was a crime. Surely you will recall what one did to the other."

I sensed Babul freeze.

"Drink his blood and eat his flesh.

"Steal his mind, sell your soul.

"Anything for power and glory over the earth.

"And the smoky, sooty world of hell...

"Shouldn't you be asking who this meddlesome interloper of my story refers to?" I interrupted myself.

Babul was very still.

"Give the name and the spell's broken," I continued, "A little ray of truth, a million tons of lies. That is how you spin the faith."

Babul's face had turned the colour of ash in wet dew.

"What do you mean by these silly riddles?" he sneered.

"Who owns the story, Babul? The weaver of myths, or the millions who bow and clap their hands?

"Or is it the greed in both that wants more and more?

"Now, what makes the moral disappear like a mist in the rising sun?"

"I see you've been dreaming," Babul began bare-facedly.

"I'm wide awake, Barwa," I called his given name. "You, rather, have been dreaming. Two hundred years of those myths that fed your power..."

For a second I thought my eyes were deceiving me. The lord himself was sweating profusely.

"There's only one trouble in your book, Babul: You underrate who we are inside, and overrate your own image in the mirror."

"You can't..." Babul practically choked like he was about to have a heart attack.

"Can't what, Babul?" I pressed on. "While you worked every angle of our fear with a tale of yesterday, today and forever, you never bargained for the other force -the light of awakened souls beaming up the universe."

"You dare the anger of your lord!" Babul's voice thundered through his mansion. But I had seen his desperation. And that was all the confirmation I needed.

"You've been dead, Babul, disembodied and not aware. They call you lord, but you're no more lord than those things by the smoky way where your pastors and mayors now find themselves..."

Then I relented with a shrug of indifference. I had made my point. It was time to leave. Babul knew that I also knew what he thought only him knew above all else. Now I felt only indifference for him.

"Keep your hood on, Babul, and tell your slaves the truth. They love you, don't they? So when they wake up becomes their morning. Bye for now. I think I can find my way out."

He was beaten.

Babul was down but not completely out, mind you. His final act would depend on the millions riveted upon his magic. Would they see the truth behind his fiction? Would they follow their intuition or just a book of tales? Would they find within their inner selves the answers they sought, or depend on priests and mayors for half truths that demean the spirit? It was up to them to choose. As for me, I had woken from a long and deep slumber. Fear and ignorance would no longer rule me. Now I was ready to savour the joy and beauty of hearts awake.

At the doorway, Babul called to me, "Friend," for the very first time.

I turned.

His horrid paws were folded across his chest. He looked deflated. The pride and arrogance were gone.

"I didn't kill my little brother," he said.

The Oracle

That was a new version.

"They said you were twins," I replied, but the old usurper brushed that one aside.

"He gave his life willingly, like all those who come to me. You see, he gave up his life for me."

"Another half-truth," I smiled to him, "but I shall proceed to pass."

And that was what I did.

Cousin waB was waiting in the hallway. He still had his damsel, the greyhound woman, by his side.

"The appointment is done with," he hazarded doubtfully as he led the way out.

"All correct," I replied.

The daemon leader betrayed no emotion. He was playing the game of knowing things before hand, their theatrics of divine omniscience. However, one thing was certain now between me and my kinsman. It was the end of muscles flexed and fangs bared against each other. For, somehow, he too knew the sign of the end when the audience no longer answered eagerly 'Oh yes!' to the rallying call of 'Story, Story!! '

waB parted the smoking blind to let me step past.

In his mind I could read the dilemma of the art that enslaved him and his fellows. Babul was their only tale of dread and might. Better to revel in the fiction that brought power, women, and everything they could dream of, than the truth that left them rather simple and with no titles to rule the world. And so let it be a long, long sleep for them that wouldn't rouse awake.

At the gate, waB paused to let me walk on through the dim chimney smoke.

"And now, each to his own world, Nwa-Bala," I called his full name. He barely managed to contain his jolt at that one. "Look now unto your house, isn't it how it's said?"

"I shouldn't forget," waB replied with a knowing wink,

stepping slowly backward to his female hound.

I was left alone to pick my way through the thickening flux of visions and the chilling noises of life-seeking creatures. Half in and out of mind I kept wondering: with the likes of Babul and his influence over us, who knows how many could prove a reliable channel for truth in a groping world?

Wide Alert

*

Now that was a costly mistake, letting my mind wander. There was hardly a warning. I did not see it before it dropped -a devastating dart that paralysed the senses and brought me instantly to my knees.

Babul!

I had underrated the con artist again, and for the umpteenth time history was about to repeat against me. How did I think he would let me out of his sphere without a last desperate fight?

Fool! I berated myself, to be demobilised by a beam, a flaring meteor of evil, an exhumation of trickery and cowardice more sickening than even the dampest graves of the lower worlds.

Then I heard their gurgling.

Babul's minions and their gibberish that mortified and made stupor of the mind!

They were tearing the life force from me, to dissipate my energy in slavish duties. I would become a nameless cipher among those millions of zombies.

I was going to die!

The realisation stampeded me to action. I began a desperate struggle to defend myself

Straining for breath, trying hard to straighten with a gasp, all effort proved useless. Many poisonous claws dug in my neck and hands and legs, tearing me to shreds. I gasped, and with a desperate, supernormal effort, wrenched both hands free. Then I began to lash wildly, hitting with all the power I could muster. My fists thumped into groggy sub earthly forms. The noises grew louder. The attack became even more vicious. I kicked and shoved. My neck had twisted at an angle that was snuffing my breath away. It was futile to battle the phantoms with fists; something impressed me to fight with hard concentration. And so with all the muscles of my will I strained against the enveloping shadows. I willed them back, commanding, holding back their psychic force, pushing against their onslaught on my existence.

Soon I felt the claw-holds weakening. Gasping for more air, I filled my lungs with vibrant energy currents that sustained life on the spheres. I felt the blessed force enliven the centres within me.

Yet success seemed minimal.

They had me still. Each time beaten off, the entities lunged back in their hundreds for the finishing attack. The darkness billowed again violently, encircling me. The noises were deafening. Then from a corner of my vision, I saw the dark creatures: weird products of once great but now diabolical minds. Quickly I willed a sword to my palm. I had nearly forgotten I could shape the force to my desire. I threw strong forceful darts. The weapon struck home repeatedly followed by loud shrieks of pain. It was my turn to grunt in satisfaction. I needed a shield. It began to form in the ether. It was now strapped firmly in my arms. I wheeled round on my feet, parrying the beaks and claws. I beat back the dark deathlike silhouettes that cluttered all over my form. I thrust through the claws of death, drawing dark and foul smells to drip into the dirt bellow.

Yet the shadows gathered, their wings flapped, hungry for more life force, desperate, impatient for the kill. Their claws lashed angrily scratching my face. I parried and dodged. I fought gallantly, beating them back. But I was losing strength while they hung on, trailing with dangerous talons and beaks. The musky smell of fear had turned them even wilder and more ferocious. There must be more than hundreds of those unearthly creatures whose stink exuded the raw devilish lust that was determined to destroy their victims forever.

Then I knew this battle was futile.

The more I fought and killed, the greater the things multiplied. Astonishing as it seemed, I was going to spend eternity fighting against a powerful malignancy that hung on and would not drop, that fed on my own fighting strength, I realised. Their own force, projected from the combination of the darkest passions of anger and greed, would never let go, would remain a permanent attachment over the aura, programmed to batter, main and whip anyone to final submission. Was this not the hypnosis of the Emperor on his fools?

I dropped my weapons.

The entities lunged forward with a lightning swoop and I was caught again in that vicious grip: limbs pulled, body torn, battered and flung into the empty space to land gracelessly on the soft murky depth below. The sharp icy beaks followed me, slashing and tearing. The life force was rapidly leaving me like water from a drainpipe. Strong talons pinned my joints to the ground. My stomach wretched in the deadly battering. A dismal smell of death filled the dark suffocating atmosphere.

Then I blacked out.

The darkness was even worse than the sharp piercing pains that shot all through the body. This was the graveyard of life; this was total stagnation at its rank. I fought the paralysis of complete psychic dismemberment. I battled my entrapment, involuntarily shuddering to imagine my fate, a zombie of Babul's, ruled by his caprice and hideous legions.

Never! There lay a far greater destiny before me. I could not afford to give up now.

I willed them back, after what seemed like aeons, commanding, holding back their psychic attack, pushing against their onslaught on my existence.

I felt their claw-holds weakening. Gasping for more air, I filled my lungs with vibrant energy currents that sustained life in the spheres. I gently asked the blessed force to enliven the centres within me.

And that was when I felt it: the light that always put an end to shadows of the damned. But in my desperation, I had forgotten that lesson with Ima and Nagua. I began to visualise it, to feel it coursing through me. It seemed an eon, an infinite length of effort and action. Then I felt it very real for the very first time.

Like a gentle wave of energy, forming through a grey veil, a tiny blob, almost weak and imperceptible against the blindfold and paralysis of hell...

Then it came breaking out.

Without warning, letting a piercing keynote which coursed the length and breadth of the darkened void, its motion, unparalleled in power, burst forth, obliterating all in its way. The streaks of heavenly fire scoured lovingly and fiercely. And in the next instant, I, Kusunku, caught in the wing of the heavens, was swirling up and up as a blinding sheet of light.

Then I was wide alert, back to the ancient mango tree.

An Open Head

*

It was still noon but seemed to be morning yet. Komas was laughing loudly and heartily. "Man, you look like you saw the ghost of Barwa himself! Don't tell me Onku's monster gave you the jitters."

Onku had an amused expression while he regarded me with a sly, thoughtful grin. Perhaps he was wondering how many heads he had opened with his tale. "Did my story scare the demon from you?" he teased.

I roused myself to look calm. I was remembering a lot of what happened and trying to reconcile them with the familiar reality that faced me now. The fire that kept us warm had burnt out completely. Only the ashes and debris remained. Onku's pipe too had since spent its billow and now rested within easy reach of his hand beside his footstool. I imagined it waiting for another moment to perform that subtle feat into the mystery of untold tales.

"You know, it's no longer your story alone, Onku, I replied. Now, it's mine as well. And I am going to do with it what I should do with it."

"No teasing," Onku laughed. "I think I've opened one head today, son of Eva. And, sooner than I thought, this bird might be ready to soar the breadths of the land."

I did not understand this last cryptic line. But I felt somehow the old man knew I was right. His taboo story had now become ours, mine, as well, to remember and, perhaps, one day, share or retell, as was fitting, with those who were ready to hear it. I was now an inheritor, one in the sacred line of the eagle clan.

Chin Ce

Yet, one thought dominated my mind, one person in the whole chain of being, and all through the chapters of the tale.

It wasn't my friend Komas and it wasn't Soda too. It wasn't the evil genius either, if you're second guessing it all. Rememb
may have swallowed more than a mouthful and, this time
was no longer a major terror of the ring as far as my life was concerned.

It was not even Nagua, as one might think. For right before me as Onku, great uncle of Komas, the old teacher had played his own part and would soon ride the wings of time into the abode of the great ancestors that had gone before him, ahead of us all on this hallowed Earth.

And we would be left only with the gift of his knowledge, and our own unique experience of it.

It was the girl that dominated my thought, the familiar being I had met within the tale but was yet to recognise in the outside world.

Out there in future time, I knew she was waiting for me.

She would be waiting for us to meet and continue from where we paused the story. I couldn't wait for the break to end.

The Oracle

THE DREAMER

Once there were three that walked together
Esther, *Patricia*, and the one called *Gee*!
To them this tale is dedicated.

Too Soon for Catty

*

She was lying on the bed, obviously having an evening rest, for her eyes were slightly shut, when he entered the narrow little corner of the hostel room that housed her bedstead.

Her corner had been kept neat; the floor was cleanly swept, her books carefully arranged on the shelf by the side of her window - except for one that stuck out an angle from the neat row.

Warily, she half opened an eye, watched him gingerly place the package of cashew nuts he had brought with him on top of her small reading table. A faint smile crossed her lips as she quickly closed it again.

They had always treated themselves to cashew or pea nuts and a drink of fruit juice, especially at the beginning of a new session, whenever he called in to take her out for a walk or to watch a play. He always bought the nuts, his favourite, and she would insist on bringing the juice, her best. Together then they made what they called their little welcome party, just for two. And she would tell him stories from the latest novel she was reading.

He looked round the room. She had done so much cleaning of the walls already. Now wallpaper of beautiful floral designs added a purple hue, an aura of homely warmth, to her side. He could notice that the spew of stickers that proclaimed Armageddon until now had somehow been purged.

One scrawled on dark green paintbrush had seriously caught his attention last semester. *Hell is Real*, it averred. Another joined: *Except Ye be born Again…* and refused to say the obvious threat. There was another famous one that read: *Education Plus Beauty Minus Christ Equal Hell Fire* -and the fire stood in the background with a red blood blaze. Beside this used to be a daring proclamation: *Beware Demons: Angels on Guard!* A riotous multitude of stickers, there used to be, plastered all over the little corner, taking up every available space as if less meant inadequacy of faith. He admired her moral strength, her courage to live up to the highest ethical standard in life, but rejected her doctrine. "Rather superfluous," he would tell her. "You'll come to know better one day."

"One day you will know, too," she would reply.

It was funny how she would turn his words on him whenever they disagreed on any one score. But he took it all in good faith. It felt like a bond between them, a feeling that was growing, and held the promise of even growing stronger in coming years after they might have left college and settled down together, stronger than the doctrine of faith that she wore like a garland around her neck. God, let that vanity go away, he had prayed. And now they were gone, all cleaned out. He really had to give God a warm hug for this one, he thought to himself.

She had certainly been busy since she returned. Quite some effort must have gone in the whole clean-out drill, and that was in spite of her long journey from home across the two great rivers. This transformation must testify to a new awakening, he hoped. "I like the decency of your corner, now," he commented, gesturing to the bright floral walls of an enchanting purple.

"Oh," she smiled wanly. "It took me one full week to dress it all up to this modest taste." She smiled again gracefully, tenderly, innocently. "And thanks."

"For what?"

"For your compliment."

"You are welcome...

"So you've been back since the week," he observed with a frown. "I thought you only returned today," he added on a surprised note.

"Ah, didn't you get my note?" she replied, adding, "on your door?"

He didn't get any note. He shook his head.

"Must have dropped off then," she said quickly.

There was something about this that struck him rather strange. It was an old trick in the book of college loves that the note dropped off the door. It was easy and convenient if you couldn't or didn't really want to keep your part of a schedule. You might even add the breeze then blew it away for good. All the chicks and dudes did that to their half brained sissies and johnnies. They called it squaring up once. But he didn't think Catty and himself would ever sidle up to that part in their dealings. At least, it was not the way they had treated each other their past three years of dating.

"Well, I'm so glad to see you anyway," he smiled looking into her eyes.

"Happy to see you, yes," she returned an uneasy laughter. After some time she asked in her warm and homely manner. "So how are the people at home?"

"Oh, they're fine. Nora sends her greetings."

"Nora.... your little sister, isn't she? How's she then?"

"Doing fine, I told her all about you," he confessed, "and she was the one who helped me post all the sweet letters I wrote you... which you never replied," he accused.

"I didn't get any letter, Dave. Oh dear, you wrote me those sweet letters like you promised?" she smiled, a wide teasing smile, and then gave him an accusing look, her pretended suspicious sideward glance that he found rather alluring. "Now what have you been telling about me?" she queried with a mischievous twinkle of her eyes.

"Well I told about us, to speak correctly."

Her eyes rounded in pretended alarm. "What about us?" she asked, eager to know.

"Well... Just that we're good friends trying to tackle our fundamental differences."

"Is that all?" she made a face of disappointment.

"No... There's more, but aren't you missing something? I can't believe you forgot our little party!" he accused. His voice was shrill with rebuke.

The Dreamer

She seemed to shrink. "Sorry, what was I thinking?" She knocked her fist on her head in gentle self rebuke. "You brought the peanuts. Ok. Let me get the juice. Just a minute, dear!" She opened her desk and rummaged for a second. Then she was off to get the fruit juice that they would use for their little get together. Everything for two. So it was agreed, and so it had always been. But how could she act now like she forgot? What had she been thinking to seem so listless on their first meeting in three months now?

He was staring into space, the way he often did when he had no answer to some puzzle that seemed to spring up without warning when his eyes fell back on one of her books in the shelf, the one that seemed to stick out of the row -like a sore thumb, he smiled. She was always adding one or more new titles to her romance list every session. He was sure she would soon be telling him some parts of the story as she read on. The title of this one was *My Prince and I.* Oh how curious. He took the book off the shelf and something tucked in between the book and another dropped to the floor. He picked it and gave a little start of surprise.

A wise man once said there were golden moments in human experience when an answer would just pop right there before you almost as soon as your question was asked. Cherish that moment, he exhorted, for it was the cosmos giving you a wink in the right direction. Dave recognised the brown five-by-seven envelope. It was the one he had used to post his holiday letters to her, only now bulky and tied with a rubber band. He did not know why he shoved the packet into his pocket. And why his heart seemed to miss a beat when he quietly replaced the book where it had stood.

Catty returned shortly carrying a pair of *Sambro* fruit juice and straws. Dave had opened the can of nuts he had set on the table. She was eager to continue from where she had left off. "So what have you been telling about me?" she queried again. There was always this naïve tone about her demands that frequently gave away her feelings or misgivings about anything. From the start he had believed this an open minded quality. It gave him the confidence to keep an open diary between them both. To Catty he was determined to be as plain and guileless as one could ever be in a relationship and she seemed to love him for it.

"You'll blush to hear the rest," he teased her.

"Try me," she laughed. Her voice was like peals of tiny bells, gentle sounds of music, in his ears.

"I'm serious," he said, trying to look truly serious and hide the smile hovering around the side of his mouth.

"So what is it? I'll try not to blush," she replied but her heart was banging crazily against her chest. She usually nursed these sudden, unexplained fears about nothing in particular and Dave would notice. It made him want to protect her, to reassure her that all was okay and that she should just be herself, no more, no less. It also encouraged him not to want to keep anything from her or do anything that might cause her to misunderstand his own loving intentions towards her.

"Well, I told her I have been crazy about you," he confessed finally, adding, "and have spent many months seeking an entrance into a heart that would not let me in for keeps." She smiled shyly and gently averted her eyes, "That's familiar..." she said, adding a trifle carelessly: "Why didn't you remember to say that you fell in love too soon for Catty..." He felt a shiver run through her body as soon as she said those words and Dave suddenly felt sick then as realisation hit home.

"Seems we are back to squaring up once," his voice was sad. "That's the word I used in the letter I wrote you, after you told me last semester that you didn't know if you loved me enough to marry me. I used it in the opposite sense, Catty dear."

"Really? I don't remember," she said hastily.

"You said 'too soon for Catty,'" Dave smiled at her. "How you have grossly understated the case at this moment?"

Even in his sadness and disappointment, he was aware her of discomfiture and decided not to press the matter further. He rather

The Dreamer

talked about other things, making a familiar joke about her grandmother and her morbid thoughts of the world coming to an end and everything returning to the dusts. And when they rather not talked, he suggested they ought to go see a movie or take a walk to the waterside. But she excused herself she was tired. So, for the first time, Dave had to retire to his room alone and unaccompanied by his beloved Catty.

An hour later, in his room, while he regarded the envelope he had retrieved from the bookshelf, the question he asked himself was *why?* Pictures and letters had been loosely strapped together. It seemed to have been done hurriedly as if the person holding them saw or heard someone coming and quickly banded everything out of sight.

It took him a long time to summon the courage to remove the loose band and take out the contents. Those were his letters all right, the three letters he had written Catty during the long vacation, and which Nora had gladly posted at his behest.

But they did not answer the question, why. What gave the answer was a familiar four by six picture she had always kept by the side of her bed. That was her cousin in the United States, she had told him. He had no reason to doubt it. Until now as he scrutinised the picture again, and another one, probably a recent one he had not seen before, which had the young man resting elegantly on a Porsche. On the back was scrawled a cursive writing that said only one word 'Sweetie.'

He smiled foolishly.

One word was all that had outmatched tons of his. *One word and a goddamn Porsche!*

He spread the first letter and began to read his own words. He had thought they were beautiful letters indeed when he wrote them because they were the first act he had ever done to completely unfold his innermost feelings to someone else -particularly in the second line of his first letter where he had made that charge of never falling too soon:

"I will never ever think, my dear, that with you I fell in love too soon," he read aloud to himself. "That would be grossly exaggerating the case. For I, who, over the years, saw nothing much to crave from the arrays of degenerating specimens of modern-age womanhood, disillusioned in what I have seen as the perpetuation of stale stereotypes, was slowly, daintily, enamoured of you, my darling.

"Mine is the slow burning fire. But it was not for them, never.

"Those Hollywood play actresses....

"Civilized in the whole confused range of mundane attitudes and imported mannerisms where a nauseating flock of bad habits had been gathered from within the worst caverns of dark minds.

"For years, darling-

"Snobbery had walked the streets, devoid of intelligence and spiritual substance, garbed in *eau de cologne* and white wash.

"Stiletto and the minis-

"Rescusitated from the embarrassing pasts of a forgotten time-

"Tap! Tap!"

"Shit and bullshit"

"Damn and F- you!

"All the vulgar specimens of an age precipitating its own debauchery in a whirlpool of misguided, obfuscated motivations-

"Were called city styles...

"And woman was transmogrified -from the natural world of laughter, and smile, and cheer, from the innocuous love of life, into a mascara of vehemence and grimace-

"And punk buffoonery!

"A smile is offensive, laughter a crime against the mock dignity of the modern trans-civilized Hollywood city star.

"Thus did this confusion walk with me, even when I met you. But I saw you and said this is the most loving woman in the whole world.

The Dreamer

"When the mountain dissolves, a land is transformed before our eyes. A new land, a new earth, ready for vegetation, ask the priest.

"Indeed, darling, the mountain loomed large then. Piles and piles of doctrines!

'From the reverend father-

'To your grandmother, there at home, where faith in the kind of love and friendship we have was all but lost.

"But who can give back what is lost; can you give what you do not have?

"So dogma had stood in the way-

"In the way of light.

"And how long did we go through all these: 'Oh Dave, I love you but I'm scared for your soul. You will lose your soul if you don't go to church!' and 'My kind of love is not exuberant or selfish. Mine is godly love, for you, Dave!'

"Honey, what is divinity? 'Fear God to save the soul,' you had said.

"I had stared at the bold letters of fear that were dipped in blood-red fires.

"Flames of torture; fires of sadistic torments.

"Which God is that but our mental projections?

"Our demonic vengeance which seeks out our weaker victims when unequally yoked together and relishes the pleasure and satisfaction, however insatiable, of devouring, manic destruction.

"Ye vindictive gods! How you have made nonsense of the love you so oft proclaimed to our mundane ears!

"And so you spoke your fears: 'I don't know how to love, how to love my God, Dave.'

"But I rejected this wicked misapplication of divine principle a long time ago.

"Priest-craft and principalities exploited the art of writing rather tendentiously. To advance their tangential doctrines!

"Love must be divine, and free. All that primitive expedition in a burning furnace is diabolism at work. And so this two-faced deity

of ours presiding over an irreconcilable dual power had made his dominance over my consciousness unacceptable. 'The soul that sinneth shall die,' your poster cries out on the wall. Each time you glanced at it again, and again, and again, your loyalty hovered.

"Dear heart, why have sin and death been their weapon of coercion for all time?

"Yet in the light we share beyond time and space, the illusion of sin and damnation evaporates. I am indestructible, I say.

"So let me eternally take on my bodies in their colours and shapes and sizes, so that experience and continuity may become the relevant element of my beingness. Let them be the purification processes of my etrnal remembering!

"Remember when you told me, with that biting sarcasm, that vehement opposition, 'Dave unbelief is the first sin in heaven and has become your own undoing!'

"For want of words, I had stared blankly into space.

"And from somewhere outside the refectory, past the silent readers in the night studiously engaged in their little corners, the noises of a frolic, a beauty contest, where the ladies displayed their pants an bras for general ogling, smacking of lips, cat calls and drooling of saliva, drifted into our silent world of deeper reflections.

"'You must be yourself,' I exhorted. 'Freedom consists not in belief but in experience!'

"'Neo-modernist,' you said...

"But what is this hypothetical concept that I advance. "Ten decades, I might say, or a hundred centuries are but passages in consciousness. Stretch time ahead. A thousand millennia in the void will hold infinite possibilities and will continue to hold gigantic advancements.

"Once upon a time painted damsels were demons and must be exorcised in deathly rituals. Today the painted beauty is the mother-goddess we often adore.

"But beauty is the attribute of a finer faculty. The dark side of human nature appropriates the negative to every good beginning. So what if I stand alone?

"And then you came up with the idea of belonging. 'A sense of belonging,' you said, 'is the security of living.'

"Yes living, maybe, but not life.

"And when I laughed derisively you said, 'I don't mind your slanderous gimmick.'

"But I had laughed because I could imagine your priest spitting fire on whoever did not belong, whoever did not bow to mammon! And why did it not surprise me?

"Long ago many were hanged for culpable heresy. It only took an accusing finger.

"Today, I have become the heretic of your faith. Would you rather then, my dear, I talked as the fanatic disciple of faith?

"I do not espouse a faith, a body of dogma founded upon unreliable mental constructions.

"I espouse love. Not fear.

"So I may not belong to that square peg of belonging. But I enjoy it. In limitless measures lies my individuality from which I can always draw my strength, lacking so much in the social cohesiveness of your sense of belonging, which you, my dearest love would rather want of me.

"I am a round peg. Round and practical. Too very wide for this world and narrow, in many cases, to sentiments -dark sentiments and ugly values.

"It might depend on how you saw it, the observer. You may have a jaundiced eye; there may be this huge log. But when vision is warped by the loudest voices of authority, who am I to yell and proffer corrections. Who am I, darling, to seek to correct ten thousand misguided watchers and idle observers in nature, the compositions of which I, even I, am borne on wings infinite; engaged in the timeless processes of understanding my complex universe.

"For whom is it complete, this world?

"So over and above this, over and above any theory of priests and principalities, all I know is this love, one with that which we seek to express in divine longing, and thus in complement with that which I seek to give you, my dearest love.

"And now, this other mountain, our faithless grands lurking in the background of two generations and brandishing their cards of images past and present, evidencing the futility of all endeavours we seek to have-

"They shall stay in the background of our landscape, our new land, our new earth.

"Hey, we cannot live our life on the ideas and considerations of our grannies. Again who can give back what has been lost; who can have what was never there to give?

"So after all these, think darling, think, and you will realize that into your tender arms I could not ever fall too soon for Catty!"

"Love, Dave."

After the first reading he suddenly felt like taking his bath and leaving the materials on his desk he reached for his plastic bucket in his wardrobe and went out to look for water.

Without a Backward Glance

*

Catty was sitting on his reading chair when he returned from the bathroom. She now had his letters in one hand, and the pictures of her cousin in the other. She was frowning thoughtfully as if weighing the importance of both objects and what each meant to her in turn. She lifted her face as he drew home the blind that demarcated his corner and bed area from the rest of his roommates'.

She was wearing an expensive brown frock upon the pair of bright red trousers her cousin had sent early that year for her birthday present. But she looked rather sickly for the very first time in his eyes now. Her chest heaved uncertainly and he could almost hear her heart, as usual, banging in fear and regret at the uncomfortable situation they had found themselves in.

On his part he felt strangely at peace, like during those midnights when lying on the bed, eyes shut in the darkness of the hostel room, half aware of the soft, uneven and sometimes harsh breathing of his roommates, he would be lost, deep in the groves of his thoughts about her.

Moreover the cold bath had relaxed him, had given him an insurgence of strength from within, which seemed to balance the right centres of his subconscious self, leaving him with a feeling of peace and goodwill. He thought this was a much welcome feeling on a moment like this.

They regarded each other for a few seconds which seemed to last for eternity. Then he broke the spell. "I see you came to take your pictures. I'm sorry I took them along with my letters," he apologised. "It was unintended. But I now know why this happened. And I am glad for the knowledge," he bit his lips and stopped.

There, he thought. He had made it easy for her to explain herself now. But she said nothing; she just sat still, weighing the objects in her hands, and feeling a shamefulness that was pathetic even for her attempy at a dignified composure. He was sorry to see her in that state and so could not ask her for any further confirmation. He already knew the obvious reason for her having to lie to him.

After what seemed several hours of disquieting silence, with Dave not going on to humour or berate as was the case in their love rows, she slowly rose to her feet, pausing half way to slide the pictures into her bag and, very gently, place his letters back on his desk.

"I'm so sorry, Davey," was all she could mutter tearfully. Then she turned and fled the room with barely a backward glance.

Feeling suddenly weak and tired, Dave no longer had appetite for dinner and no interest in prep for the night. He just wanted a sleep right there and then, a sleep that would blot out the whole damned scene from his mind. Minutes later, he changed into his pyjamas and flopped onto the low metal bunk.

Rather than blot anything out, his thoughts that night were of her and all they had done in the past. She was now resting on the bed while he sat on the chair facing her, and sipping from the bottle of coke she had offered him.

He had just done justice to his share of the chicken she had cooked. It remained the bones and little bits of flesh which he was busy picking slowly with his teeth. Then he drained the bottle of its contents and pushed the plate a little further away.

"Such generosity," he grinned and licked his lips to show his relish, "doesn't come quite often. For which I am so grateful." She smiled her lovely smile, looking beautiful in an expensive green satin gown, which showed her firm bust in a modest way. "I'm happy you enjoyed all of it," she said.

"Sure, the meat was very good."

"Thanks for liking it," she picked the bottle and plate away.

"Wonder why we don't see much of these where we live," he remarked.

"Because the boys cannot afford it," she teased.

"Or their eating habits are more disciplined," he returned.

He stared at the familiar pictures on the desk, a small portrait of her at one, and that of her cousin at the other end. Both were framed in steel. He was always fondly looking at her bright and brilliant eyes, the wide set lips on which he can read a great deal of determination, and the tenderness of her pose which brought a smile of adoration on his face every time he contemplated her.

He watched a large mosquito fly and hover around the frame, and impulsively struck, knocking the picture off the desk. Quickly, delicately, he picked it up rubbing off a stain that was not there. "Guess I nearly killed it," he said.

"Our windows have no gauze," she gestured. "So it seems they all come to feed here."

"You should complain to the porters," he advised.

"We have done that; they say it's the job of Works... and Works say it is the duty of Admin to inform them... So nothing has been done since." She opened her wardrobe, and brought out a tin of *Baygon* insecticide, shaking it vigorously. "We use this meanwhile."

"And what do you want to do now?"

"Spray a little, do you mind? I know it can be unpleasant."

He shrugged in agreement, adding "And unhealthy."

"We will go out for a walk," she suggested, "and the smell would have gone when we return."

"Fine then," Dave said, rising to his feet, and holding his breath as the pungent spray hit his nose.

It was dark outside, already night, he found to his surprise, and then realised how long he had spent in her room. Probably over three hours, he guessed. For just that brief stay with her!

"How time flies when I'm with you," he told her. She nodded, smiling.

"I often wonder about that too."

"Well, it gives me great joy," he confessed. "For once in my life, I never can get bored; it's a very special feeling."

She nodded again, looking into the distance ahead.

Hands linked, they took the flower garden path that led away from the female hostel, walking very slowly, enjoying each pace forward and nowhere in particular. The path led toward the football stadium further from the campus where the lights of the hostels became only dull glints away in the distance.

They made their shelter under a lone *yaro* tree by a grassless corner near the roadside. It was cosy, warm and comfortable with each beside the other.

They spent the remaining hours of night there, sitting thus for a long time, feeling the warmth and throbbing of their hearts, and the contentment known to only them both. The moon, their favourite companion this time, was near full, shining warmly, a sedate matron in the centre of the bright clouds floating cooly in the airy endless space of the spheres.

He remembered a previous moment, their last night together before the close of the semester, here on the some lovely spot under this tree. They had watched the stars sparkle from the dark unknown distance as she sang an old, familiar song that brought a yearning and longing from within his deepest heart. It was a song about, two friends, two truthful lovers, somehow helping each other through the hard times.

And she had taught him the song -rather the refrain which was all that mattered when he listened to her mellow enchanting voice over and over until he was carried away in an emotion of indescribable thrill, joy and strange pain. And over the days, even at the distant north where he spent a dreary vacation, he tried to relive the very moments of that experience, the tightness that gripped him around the chest, as he listened to her, searching her eyes for a message of true love in that song...

"Our moon is growing full again," he observed in a warm

husky voice.

"Very nearly," she remarked, "it will be full moon yet."

Together they watched the bright luminescence of the heavens, savouring the elegance of the brilliant golden hue cast around the active night, watching the dark silhouettes of the trees and the roofs of houses far away in the town, barely visible from their lonely position under the *yaro* tree. And the steadiness of their gaze yielded in a single blur with the clouds and the moon, and the golden landscape of the night, and the darkness and lonely silence of the world around them, punctuated by the sound of their own voice and the noise of the night insects.

"Some times like this I'd want a home in the moon," she said, laughing at herself. "How would you like it Davey?" her voice had an affectionate ring to it.

"Just the two of us?" he asked.

"Of course, silly. Were you thinking of a politician with you on the moon?"

He smiled and answered: "That would be lovely... except maybe it would be lonely... without people."

"It would be warm... who likes a swarm of people in the first place."

"Well there's this idea of life in the moon," Dave told her.

"Like we have here on the planet?"

"It's little better at one end, a little worse at the other... with and witchcraft, deception and wars, so the legend goes."

"Then we will live at the better end..."

He agreed. "Life there is nobler than anything on earth," he continued. "There's creativity, there's love, and there's harmony, like in Venus of the golden music."

"So how do we catch a flight?" she teased with practical enthusiasm.

"No we travel soul-wise," he laughed. "It's faster than light... and we can explore further planets and worlds.

"And maybe talk to the man with the axe," she added with a

laugh. "He defied the day of worship and made God angry. So He put him there to serve as a lesson to others." They laughed warm heartedly.

"My sister really made me believe that story. So every Sunday, I always have to go to church," she recalled with a smile.

"In our village, the fellow was first turned to stone then taken up there."

"Maybe the stones the astronauts picked where they landed," she mused. "Do you also wonder if moon-dwellers fear the UFOs the way we do here."

"No," Dave replied sagely. "Extraterrestrials must be great friends with the people there."

She heaved a deep breath, pulling him by the arm with a warm contended sigh.

"Sing me to sleep Davey," she cooed, "I feel so happy and cosy with you."

He pulled her to him and she snuggled into his arms, her eyes glowing and dancing as they came together in a long deep kiss...

After what seemed a brief moment in eternity, she stirred her body, hitting weakly at the leg where a mosquito had bitten her then cuddled back into his arms.

He massaged her affectionately. She opened the eyes she had shut in the darkness, her mind rested in the deepening silence of the night, or was it the dawn? Finally it was she who said, "we should be going, Dave."

"Yeah," he agreed weakly. "We have nearly spent the whole night here."

"Do you think it's dawn now? It's so cold and chilly." She rose to her feet shivering and moving closer to shield her body with his. And he offered his hands around her neck; his coat covered her back as they walked backed to the hostel, slowly, happily, in the quiet silent night of the sleeping world.

At the door, she stopped to kiss him goodnight and they clung to each other again, he looking into her beaming face, into a pair of eyes that danced with sheer delight!

"Good morning," she announced ironically and they laughed in bemusement at themselves.

"Funny enough, I don't feel tired," he said.

"Me too."

"So let's stand like this till the day breaks," he proposed.

Her eyes rounded in alarm. "We will give some porters the shock of their lives," she giggled, lifting her hands to her head and feeling her hair. "That reminds me, I'll be going to plait my hair tomorrow... I've nearly forgotten to tell you."

"Not bad," he cooed. "I'll love your new look, even though I'd miss your low cut."

She smiled. "It's just for only one week or two... You'll come with me, won't you?'"

"Go with you!" he made it sound unthinkable, but it didn't produce the effect he wanted. She continued, coolly ignoring his objection. "Yes... later we'll go to class... Oh today is Sunday. The salon won't open. Sorry I forgot. Then we go to church," she sang along. "Now don't tell me you'll be running to any meeting again, Davey, we give the day to church... And you are not going anywhere else," she concluded finally, her hands on her hips in a mock aggressive posture.

She stopped soon enough and glanced at him, flashing a brilliant smile.

"You are beautiful," he told her. The compliment knocked her wide-mouthed. Her eyes rolled twice over.

"Dave! You are unpredictable!"

"Yes?" he grinned triumphantly.

Her iris caught the light of the bulb and glew like two beautiful stars; it lighted the clear white of her eyes.

"Saying things at the wrong time," she remonstrated

"Well, doesn't matter as long as it is the right thing." He smiled into her eyes, those clear, frank, and loving eyes, while she fondled with the neck collar of his shirt.

"Thanks for your compliment, but it doesn't kill the matter of church, remember?" she gave a winning nod, with a vigorous motion of her head that was child-like and alluring in the loveliness of her gait.

She had true warmth, such glowing warmth which held no affectations and drew him on and on to the very core, the very centre of her heart.

It was a feeling he had, and which he was yet to admit to a living soul.

No, not one.

For that special feeling, that trust and confidence in the veracity of his deepest convictions, the pricelessness of this rare gem, must be guarded, relived and rewon like God's kingdom itself; yeah, not scattered, not thrown onto the dirts of trivial light talk.

So he had thought.

Beautiful Letters

The room was hot and stuffy. He realised he was sweating and his hands were shaking. A strange vision of dad came to his mind as he watched his hands. As a child he used to watch dad read his mails every night while he held the *Feuer Hand* lantern for him. Dad's strong, hairy hands would be dancing slightly in the pale light as he read the scripts, his sharp intelligent eyes sweeping the contents in each brief moment of scanning while his lips mumbled one or two occasional remarks about the message or the penman. He was feeling like dad now, he smiled to himself.

It was getting rather hot for the night, he said in his mind. The ceiling fan did not seem to help too. He looked round and saw why. All the window louvres were shut. That must be the work of Papy-Jay his roommate. Why was he always doing that? Shutting off the air in a hostel room of eight occupants always seemed horrible to all but Papy.

He stood to open the louvres near his corner, inhaling the soft stream of the cold night air on his face.

He had the second letter in his hand now: the one where he argued on the indissolubility and inseperability of their souls. His beautiful letters, he smiled wanly and read again.

"Dearest Love,

"I am looking at your picture as I write. After this one, there may not be another chance before school resumes. Remember I promised three mails this holiday, and you also said you'd do the same. Well, I won't wait to get your reply before I complete my turn, not when I feel you here next to me smiling in that uncertain way you always seemed to look at me!

"Anyway, having your picture and staring at it, it offers me a little bit look at myself from a big room space. This experience of self-expression is a kind of standing out and taking stock of the inner motivations and actions around my life. And I find within this experience an understanding and faith and strength that surpasseth all.

"I discover a loyalty that can never be displaced even in the face of the storms and forces that shake its existence. And above all, a unique feeling defying, surpassing all the logical ratiocinations and social traditions of a society that scorns and threatens to dissolve the authenticity of other ways and universes of being.

"This second discovery can be startling. I used to think I was all alone in this experience, but one day I overheard my dad discussing a similar matter with his best friend Nat. I must have felt like Elijah in the wilderness then. But 'over there,' God had told him, 'are a band of others like you.'

"To reconcile our own paradox is the challenge of our world of silent lives. Love can be found in the humblest of hearts, in the noblest of places where snobs and arrogant fools march past for futile adventures in their desert of empty lives.

"So alone we are, and faith moulds up immense, endless worlds of love and joy and happiness, silently and secretly!

"Our happiness is my reality, darling, my reality that is changing with the states and perspectives with which we look at ourselves and the world.

"The world of that small band like me, over there and maybe around here, I may not tell, but the thread, unseen, has linked our dreams, within a country and a planet beyond space and time.

"Therefore, my dearest, my love is of the golden heart that casts a humming light over and above the clouds, the suns, the moons and the stars of our lives in the dark nights of the slumbering world.

"You called it 'transcendental'-

"And so shall it be: beyond the dregs and narrow alleys of material worship, above the destructive reach of slander and distortion, beyond all ignoble intents in this devalued world. Yet full of energy, promise, and the vital force of our minds is the spirit of our love.

"And dearest, I see myself, -you and me- one with this overwhelming force that has directed and controlled the minute levels of our lives, even to the beating of our hearts, and our ultimate unfolding into the paramount awareness of ourselves within the worlds of our being.

"Let us carry it along the corners of the rowdy streets, the busy express-ways, and the far flung country sides. Let it be there and here, with us, throughout the tensions and the foibles of our existence. And even in those minute fears and consequent angers, misunderstandings, and other subtle forces we set in motion, let it be there, seeking right balancing and harmony, and placing us in more situations that light up our of creative awareness of our life. Together or not.

"How unrecognisable to the rabble is the subtlety of this one force that binds us all, my beloved.

"Which makes it even the more amusing when, wrapped joyfully within the secret chambers of our hearts, we watch those who, stunted by lack of faith and, spurned by their loveless minds, make a mockery of attempt to place a finger onto what we have.

"You know who we mean, don't you darling?

"But the sincerity of our motives, of our quests, is what we really have, yet who will accept to make this-

"The light and beauty of the innermost core?

"'God dwells in the most secret place within your hearts,' say the wise angels.

"In our secret hearts, darling, in our secret world of our dreams, the doors shall be barred to furtive glances and prying eyes, to the curious little monkeys that leap around the trees, to a jeering loveless crowd that yell: 'Conform and be like us!'

"Even the silence speaks vast spheres of possibilities to hearts that reach for the heights of love, to souls who dream in vast worlds of colour and light.

"Herein, my love, our reality lies, expanding with this infinite awareness of ourselves, and of what we have; the faith and love we have deeply sown on our meeting and the union of our hearts, will mould, forever protected, an unbroken matrix into the secret heavens of our life!

"Love, Davey"

The tiny digital clock on his reading desk made a short, dull click of the hour. He saw it was eight. He would round off the reading and catch his dinner. It was going to be a lonely prep after. Slowly, he placed the second letter on top of the first and, heaving a deep sigh, began to read the third.

It was brief. He must have been in a hurry to fulfil his promise of writing her three letters. It was strange as he saw it now. He was rather more anxious that she got his three mails than he cared about receiving her replies. And gratefully now, it was the letter, the completion of the process of unburdening, of disclosure, that was responsible for bringing things to light. He read on with a wry smile:

"My darling,

"Happily, here is the third letter I promised you -although I am yet to receive your own! But I do not mind. The knowledge that you got all of mine in good health is more important to me.

"Besides, by the time this letter gets there you should be preparing your journey back to school, back to the days and moments I have spent the last six weeks reliving in my mind.

"Those days, my dearest darling, are like adventures in the dream worlds.

"Though the struggle to understand ourselves, breaking away from those who will quote long verses of damnation from outdated books, breaking away from the daily onslaught on our consciousness the frightening philosophy of our parents: 'Ash thou art, so love is ash as all to ash returneth.'-

"Though the struggle was long, and wracking on our nerves, love had walked by our side, keeping silent company, and patiently, softly, had revealed to us the unfolding promise of a life of devotion and trust and faith. Love is the beginning and the ending of all the lives that can be lived.

"So how much do they know? Those who know all the doctrines of the prophets and the saints and the saviours, those who have imbibed all the philosophies and prophecies of this world, how much do they have? How much do they have of this love that can only be given and shared?

"In our deepest hearts, my love, lies not the faintest flush of regret for what we have sought, all that we have given, and everything that we have done in expression of this one love....

"So walk with me in this moment of reflection to the riverside where we had our first picnic. The river had risen to the brim, this evening, by the low valley of the farm where the cassava plants made a delightful shade, the nest, under which we had lain, side by side on the little mat you had brought for this lovely evening alone, and safe, the two of us.

"And we had lunch, the yam and tasty stew you had cooked also for this lovely event of our life. I ate from your lovely hands as you fed the bits into my mouth.

"Content with the world, within the silent hearts of the bush, the old mounds of the farms and the cassava leaves that rustled lightly in the gentle breeze, we played hide and seek and wrestled on the ground.

"Then spent from the sheer length of our game and our wild laughter, you laid back to rest under the shade of leaves.

"Long after, the evening was fast, the sun, a bright orange ball was making her journey toward the western skies, and it was time for us to go.

"I tried to pull you up, reluctant as you seemed, then I planted, without warning, the kiss I long yearned to give on your red warm lips. I watched your closed eyes, in your relaxation, for a sign.

The Dreamer

"And you slapped me right then straight on the face, your eyes still closed, while your face left little of any sign I had sought.

"But as we walked back to the hostel, your hands gently clasped in mine, picking our way past the mounds of the farm and the cassava plants and shrubs, we knew, although silently, in this unspoken feeling, that our fate had been sealed by the love and faith we had written that evening into our hearts…

"Oh, come back soon, my love, for I miss you dearly.

"Your Davey."

Enough for Two

For several days after they parted ways, Catty always appeared in his mind. Or he it was who carried his little box of memories of them both, her lovely, uncertain smiles that lighted every little corner they sat, and their little lonely walks to everywhere and nowhere, with she sometimes staring at him with reddening eyes, grinding her teeth in mystified silence, and stepping jerkily like a cat that had treaded water.

When suddenly those eyes would turn all red, bloodshot, as if her mysterious cycle had started to flow and was letting it all loose upon her eyes, he would ask in quick anxiety: "what's wrong dear?" But all that came back was silence, and that strange chattering of her teeth. Alarmed and pulling her close to examine her, she would fling into his arms, her feverish body melting into the energy of a healing power that lay in their long and deep kiss.

This was one of those moments when it was going to be Sunday and they had preferred to spend their Saturday night alone by themselves in a cosy far off corner of the main campus block. There they watched as the night made its dying sighs in the cold airy darkness. And when all had got real quiet, as if waiting for the dawn to begin to rouse in the silent deadness of night, they walked slowly down to the hostel quarters. He had his protective right arm over her neck and she her left hand around his waist as they sauntered and stopped by the awning to bid each other good night.

She felt very warm in his arms as he kissed her and, gently, with great reluctance, relaxed his grip on her waist.

"Now you go and get some rest before the remaining hours break into day," he told her.

And she smiled, nodding her head, her lips widening with amusement.

"Yes, before we begin to sleep on each other's arms.... Imagine anyone coming out and seeing this young couple clasped together and sleeping on their feet."

"Beautiful spectacle," he replied.

"Oh Dave!"

He led her toward her hostel door but she pulled back.

"I'll see you off to the road... just a little, *please,*"

"After which it'll be my turn to walk you back here again."

"And we'll be walking to and fro until daybreak... which will be crazier than standing in a corner," she laughed. "Come to think of it Dave," she mused, "that's what we did the night of the riot, remember? You walked me to the door three times...and I saw you off thrice again! And when you left, there was this guy following you behind. I got alarmed that he was up to some harm, so I stalked him too."

"Yeah," Dave laughed. "And that was how you landed back to my hostel in that unholy hour, looking red in the eyes. And I had to walk you home again."

They walked slowly down the road with his hand around her neck and hers on his back, the night as still as silence itself. A light, cold wind brushed softly against their cheeks as they walked back again to stop by the gated columns of her hostel.

"You really have to go in now," he said.

"Yes sir," she threw her arms around his neck, lifting slightly to give him a peck on the cheek, which felt so warm in the cold night. "Don't worry. I won't bother to follow you again," she added with a lovely smile, and a determined look in her eyes.

"I love you."

"I love you too."

Standing by the corner of the road like a statue, he watched her retreating back. He wore a tender expression on his face and a transparent gleam in his eyes.

Chin Ce

She walked with light easy steps, with the grace and confidence of a doll completely at ease with herself and everything around her. At the front door she paused, pushing the glass door with her left and turning to give a gentle wave.

"Goodnight, darling," he whispered. He could feel the smile on her lips from where he stood; he felt it reaching out to him like a warm embrace overflowing with joy. He waved back with all the love in his heart then turned to walk quickly, jauntily, toward his own hostel.

Dave was in tears. How her presence, even as he lay on his side, his pillow snuggled in his arms, filled his mind, his thoughts, his whole consciousness then, as if nothing else mattered in the world but that subtle force that had brought them together.

It was enough for him, the force; he believed it had always been there, even without his conscious awareness of it, and had directed his personal life, from his dreams to the most casual events in his life.

So that when he cast his mind back, shuffling through the images of past events to their first meeting in the car, it appeared as if some time in a previous existence that preceded their present life, they had agreed to meet there and then, under that most casual and fleeting circumstance....

It was hot inside the Peugeot 504 wagon that they had struggled and clawed to clamber onto. He now detested those moments of life and death battle in the jungle world of men and women -simply over boarding a cab.

Formerly, he had liked being counted among the strongest of them that always won the survival of the fittest game. Until one day an unforseen shove did the job, and down he went onto a nasty pile of mud dirt. It was then he learned that the fight was not worth the fall afterall.

Instead he learned another way: he would stand at a corner,

The Dreamer

alert and watching the confusion, the swarm of bodies shoving and pushing. Sometimes, a narrow opening beckoned from the closure, and very quickly, he would stoop and slip himself in, effortlessly through the exertion of bodies to find a place.

That day had been a long wait before he managed to get into a cab. Under the glazing February sun how his patience had stretched! He wound down the glass a little bending over the girl sitting by the door. His hand brushed slightly against her breasts in the process and he found himself stuttering profusely, "Sorry... Sorry please." He held his breath as her eyes fluttered briefly, and then, she flashed him a warm reassuring smile. "It's ok.," she said.

He breathed in relief.

"Tough day, huh?" he gestured. "We are lucky to manage a seat."

"Yah," she smiled gratefully, "Lucky somehow."

"Women are always lucky," he teased. She laughed good-naturedly.

"It's providence... We could have roasted in that heat!"

"It's a miracle," he agreed.

"That's true."

He had begun to like her then, struck by her easy nature. Her face had a radiant air; there was a warm kind of pull about her.

"Seems we're heading the same place," she smiled to him.

"Campus?" he lifted an enquiring eyebrow.

"Yes," she replied.

"I thought as much. It's always causing the rush..."

They began to chat about the events of the last session, particularly the violent student demonstrations.

The next time they met, in a bank, he recognised her first as she walked briskly and noiselessly in a pair of brown canvas shoes and a light feathery gown to the glass cabin. Her hair was tucked into a black cap. Dave thought she looked beautiful. He watched her luscious lips as she filled a slip of paper, noting a strange kind of excitement forming inside his heart.

Minutes later, she turned, her bright eyes searching for a place to sit among the waiting customers. Her eyes fell on his. He stared back awkwardly, and then happily, as she fluttered her eyes in recognition and moved over to him. He made a place for her which she gladly took.

"I thought you wouldn't recognise me," he confessed with a chortle that was also apologetic.

"Not after I have had a chat with you," she laughed.

"But most wouldn't care to show that they even remembered," he insisted.

"Well... you've said *most,*" she replied, shrugging her shoulders in an expressive manner. "I am not *most.*"

He felt suddenly warm by her side in spite of the chill in the air-conditioned banking hall.

"I thought of checking you up in your hostel the next evening," she revealed, "only that, funny enough, I didn't get the number of your room or even the name of my first acquaintance."

"How is that?" he asked, foolishly. "You mean you were really going to pay me a visit?"

"Why not?" she smiled.

Here at last, he thought, was the one: a woman without a mask, just being herself. But wasn't this just what he had been looking for? Somewhere in his subconscious mind and his subtle dreams, even in his growing disappointment and conscious distaste for the clowns of Hollywood, there was a search. Somewhere in his proud refusal to extend any bit of the silly play acting of society beyond the regular norms of formal courtesies, he had looked out for the beautiful one, the golden hearted priestess of the sun that would rise and set daily in his heart.

"It would have been most beautiful to have you around," he said with genuine feeling.

"Really?" she smiled again. "Then I'll be looking you up next time -to bring you to our fellowship," she added.

The Dreamer

His heart sank a little on realising the purpose of her coming, but recovering, he assured her sincerely with the reply: "That would be my pleasure."

"Only that I still don't get the name at all," she said with a laugh. "Funny how we have known each other without even an introduction."

"And what's with all that anyway," he replied. "I deem it lovely that way round. We found the substance of knowing before the formalities of meeting."

"Hm, that's an interesting argument," she conceded. "I think I'll buy that."

"Good then," he smiled. "I am David, named after my ancestor Tuthmosis III, the David, the pharoah, and mightiest of all the kings of the ancient world." Just then the teller clerk called 'David Oje!'

"You see," he smiled, "there's really more to the name."

She giggled as he rose to his feet. "You're quite a funny person. I am Catherine, but my friends call me Catty."

That had marked the start of a romantic affair. Soon he was often seen with her; they were always walking and holding hands, teasing and laughing at each other. They had always walked somewhere and everywhere in strange and familiar places...

*

In his dream they boarded a long bus packed with people travelling and returning from their journeys. She was half-sitting on his laps; her hands were clasped tenderly around his waist. The vehicle must have hit a great pothole and Catty had bumped right off his lap and onto the floor.

When he woke to the early morning sunlight, lying still for a moment to recall and contemplate his dream, then leaping up energetically to start his morning, he tried not to feel her presence around and within his whole being anymore. It was going to be difficult but there seemed no other way. Life had thrown him a curve ball but as their local highlife singer had said it, 'when your

Chi brings you a gift load of hard-luck, to whom would you pass it on?'

He had a cold quick shower, dressed for class, and then had his favourite breakfast of tea and egg. The letters were still lying on the table when he hitched his backpack and readied to move on. He took the letters and thought for a moment, then tore them into tiny bits and shreds and threw in the bin.

Until that morning, it was always a happy feeling when the morning sun, steadied beyond the clouds, lighted the earth brilliant and clear for another exciting day, because he knew she would be there by the hallway waiting for him and humming that tune about their building a bungalow big enough for two.

The Oracle (web anthology version)

I

IT was near noon but seemed to be morning yet. Koma's uncle reclined by his choice corner before the veranda of the house under the shade of an ancient mango that now looked like a baobab tree warming his legs by the hearth. He had just lectured us against our silly game of cards and rounded off a familiar one about one of his travels round the world. Now he contemplated his pipe with a curious expression on his face. Komas and I pestered for another story.

"Onku, what can you tell us about the legend of the Kongo twin," I ventured.

The December harmattan blew a stream of chilly bursts that scattered leaves and dusts. This season's was the strong type that would dry your skin brittle and freeze your bones if you let it. It brought nostalgic memories of my childhood that carried further to some distant and forgotten period in a dim past.

"Barwa or Parwa?" the old teacher frowned; his brows and moustache were etched white. "That story is well untold. Sunu, son of my good friend, Eva," he called to me, "Why do you want to know things that should not be told to young ears?"

"A great teacher once said that the lore of old could tell where the rain began to beat us," I feigned.

"Surely, your memory has not failed you, Onku?" Komas shot him a glance and we exchanged furtive smiles. We knew how to pull the leg of the grand master. Wonder aloud if his memory was failing and you had him. For Onku and his travels round the world made irresistible stories for anyone who had ears to listen.

He was a glorious old fellow, though well in his eighties now. His face had an unnatural tinge behind the hardened, marbled eyes that had looked fear and death in the face many times over. This great bird of our clan had known years of rare wisdom which the young, as he often said, had yet to understand.

"Barwa and Parwa," he said again. "-the big lie of history; one black like coal, the other fair like ripe pawpaw," he smiled to himself. It was as if a chapter of the story was lighting up in his memory. "After them, none could have twins again in the whole of Kongo...

"That was until Slessor came!

"Of course, there are other versions," he acknowledged. "Some say they were not twins but brothers. Others that they were close friends, you know, 'five-and-six,' like you and Okoma," he gestured good naturedly to his great nephew who had a different kind of smile on his face as he anticipated the old man.

Onku - the way we called him - was actually the great uncle of Komas and had become the oldest surviving member of the family as well as the entire clan of Omaha. It was said that Onku went to Cambridge but his unlettered grandfather, Aham, the great seer of Omaha, was the one who opened his head and placed the ancient knowledge of the clan in them.

"Yes, I still have my memory intact," Onku had warmed to the bait. "And which one of you shall claim it when I pass on? ...that is, if chickens will ever come to cockerels for guidance. Ha! Ha!"

We laughed with him.

"Oh yes," he continued on his usual gay note. "Only the old can tell an original tune. But first, you must make me my pipe, Oko," he commanded. "And you, Sunu, stir the fire to warm my bones!"

Komas still had the knowing smile on his face as he hastened to oblige him while I gathered the tinder to revive the dying hearth.

Onku nudged me with a gay chuckle, showing a whole pair of toothless gums save few brown and rusted molars. "Really," he teased, "you boys waste your time with those cards you call a game," he peered into my face. "College these days is a pack of cards, isn't it?"

"No, a load of books," I corrected with equal humour. "Many

books and quizzes, you know."

"Baa!" he snorted. "And what do those chap books tell? Blind as bats and leading their young to the ditch. Baa!" he shuffled both feet on the ground. "If you learned at the feet of the oracle, you would come to know the true wisdom of Mother Earth, I tell you."

Presently Komas was back with the pipe refilled just the way the old man liked it - with a trail of white cloud. Onku would tell you he had tended those herbs since his young days, even after his Cambridge and before his travels; in fact, from time immemorial. Soon he was puffing luxuriantly, sending out brilliant sparks of light accompanied with dull thuds of crackling seeds. His eyes glowed as he let the smoke drift through the chimney of his nostrils and ears. Then he blew straight to my face. I winced and made as if to cough, holding my breath. This was the part he seemed to like for he gave a loud chortle. "You must smoke a pipe one day, boy," he told me. "Learn to open up your mind. Now where were we?" he asked.

"Barwa and Parwa," Komas reminded him.

"The big lie of history," I added.

"The tale is taboo," he warned again; "might turn your head when you hear it. And no," he raised his right hand and his wizened index finger dug into my chest. It felt like a sharp sting from a talon. "Only one survived: Barwa, or Babul the great, who seized the life force of his twin and lived for seven whole generations!" he motioned.

Then his voice began to sound like a tape about to fast forward. "Some say he never died but still lives, a phantom of a life-" he winked knowingly.

"The sort that, rather than go on in the land of the ancients, falls back to the abyss, the darkness of the void, to become an incarnate of Enshu himself-

"Enshu," he smirked, "who never tires of the chase nor wearies of the hunt..." he paused. His hairy nostrils and lips were barely visible in the white cloud from his pipe.

"And we in this land, my boy," his eyes, presently blood shot

The Oracle

with mysterious gleams, dug into mine. I had a sickening feeling in the pit of my stomach as his voice took on an eerie note.

"We are the quarry. Ha! Ha! Ha!"

My head was swelling, dizzy with unearthly gurgles and foggy visions that seemed to jog my body of memory alert.

Or numb?

Whatever the case, I must have been completely unprepared for what followed next...

*

Suddenly I was running.

Fast as the wind, fast as my thoughts, all seemed lost in the blur; the entire world had fled with a rapidity that astonished me. Only the sound of the wind cooed sharply and furiously against the ears as I ran along a dusty road, blind and not looking.

I must have been running for hours, maybe days. My breath was beginning to flail. My lungs stung; my belly was a violent ache as if something was lodged in my mid-section. I lurched violently, reeling left and right, my legs sagging from underneath me. Finally, I came down with a slow, weary slump, blacking out the fast receding world I fled from.

When my eyes opened again I found myself in a secluded corner of a wide desert, near a bare footstone among some dusty piles of rock. This was strange. Where was I?

It's Naigon, I realised. Here was the arid region so much talked about in Kongo legends where battles had taken place in human heads. Stretched ahead were the desert and sand mounds of an endless, sprawling wasteland. The sand and dusts swirled and danced in wild gyrations to surging winds.

"To be free at last," I found myself muttering, although not knowing why I said that. Maybe it was the feeling of vastness and space in this region that had impressed itself upon me as I rested to meditate upon the prospect of tearing free from the sudden blight.

For everywhere around me was yawning poverty and scorched parches of stone. The sun had become a never-setting glaze of terror, its countenance a fierce tinge of devilish vengeance upon this part of earth that seemed impervious to all noble intents.

I began to thirst. Beads of perspiration were dropping down my neck. I shut my eyes. I had a long history behind, and a promising task ahead.

The wind was lashing violently like a discarnate monster. Its deathly hand seemed to lace over my head; a sense of foreboding hovered ever so near. I was way to a past that was stealthily pulling me by the ears. I was seeing images of terror and, I knew, somehow, they were projected by a virulent power in a matrix of thought forms. The muscles of my eyes were hurting from the strain of keeping them tightly shut from these spectres of my imagination. It was a great effort to keep still in that terror and not let out a yell and bound away to any ever place. Sit still, shut it tight, and do not give away your hiding place with much of a whisper was what I told myself.

But out of the dark emerged a head, or what looked like a hound. Its teeth were barred, the lips curled in a snarl. It was hunched double as it sniffed the air. Its paws, hung limply from a gnarled hairy chest, made careless patterns on the ground. Our eyes met. I recognised him immediately as he gave a long growl of vicious temper. waB! That dreaded messenger of Babul and chief of his staff of minions!

"So there you are!" he barked in that taut manner of his liege. "You thought you could escape the power of my arms, didn't you?"

My fear was full blown in one fleeting, paralysing moment. And then it was gone, made way for the contempt I had for the likes of these guards that were now emerging from beneath the sands.

"I have come a long way," I replied, feeling a surge of strength welling from within. Surely, this new wave of energy could not be mine, I thought. It was as if some higher power had quickly impressed through my head, arms and fingers the power to fight at that moment where I had my back to a wall of sand. And all I needed to do was stretch a long and defiant arm that would summon the light to an explosive battle with my enemies. But it was obvious that this struggle involved a severe force I had not quite understood. So the balance of power was tilted against me. Even so, "I have come a long way, waB, I am not going back there, I said again."

The hound was cast in the character of his lord. waB believed himself prince as his master was king. Their masks would haunt anyone, anywhere -those visages of terror and darkness robbing peace from the soul. And here in the blazing desert must one also strain and fight -all for the good purpose. Peace was, indeed, our purpose of coming to live on Mother Earth since the first beginnings...

These uncommon thoughts raced through me in milliseconds. It felt like an intense downpour, and they were pouring from a deep source within although I knew not where.

"We are here to take you back," waB said again, with very little patience, adding finally: "to where you belong."

"See who has come to tell me where I belong," I retorted, but mine was with calmness, perfectly within the presence that had given me this serene composure to face my captors, I mused, just as waB's eyes turned angry flashes of blood red. "Don't be silly," he snapped, "You belong back to where you fled. Now let's go. You are enough disgrace to your fellows. Baba was there; he came personally in the midst of the congregation to welcome you..."

"Stop, you moron!" I suddenly yelled. "Stop parroting that murderous beast. Surely, waB, this web is not a life for you or me. We must stop; we must quit that den, or lose our selves to hopeless evil."

waB only wrung his neck leftward and rightward, and then leant forward with a leering grin. "I knew you wouldn't give easy," his visage changed as he straightened his muzzle. "Take him!" he thundered. His eyes were his lord's firework, the smell of his breath, straight in my face, like carbon belching. The rest of them who had laid back now began to emerge from both sides, eyes in flame, lips curled, fangs barred; their measured stealthy walk, their single determination exuded from the virulence and meanness for which waB and his league were famous.

Rough paws jabbed at me from left and right. I felt like being torn to pieces by a hundred jaws, then flung hopelessly into an abyss of darkness and nothingness.

I woke up to find myself face to face with the dreaded lord of the realm. My legs and wrists seemed bound and spread apart. I was left hanging in space or floating upside down in a helpless, perplexing manner. The great Babul himself was dressed like a mediaeval warrior as he paced the air. His face was the colour of soot smeared thinly over a bony skull that brought instant revulsion as he gazed at you through chilly dead coals that served for eyes. His hands were folded behind his back. His huge black and red drape was hung down his shoulders, sweeping the floor and covering a pair of hinds ensconced in black leather boots.

"I brought you in," he started with condescending friendliness... and a pause-

"So that you can fully appreciate the seriousness of the dilemma before you-

"And the enormity of my power!" he spat violently.

He let a few seconds pass, and then spoke again.

"Prodigal, there is no running from the lord and master of the realm, in search of what? Wisdom? Moral? Which is better: to flee the thrall of my presence and then incur my wrath upon your head, or come willingly into my acts with all pleasure guaranteed..."

The unwilling quarry and the ruthless hunter, I sighed.

It was going to be a long and hopeless torture. I quietly helped myself to a passage in gentle comatose...

But there was to be no escape from the hypnosis of fear and desperation that had made captive of my mind and body. Babul's

The Oracle

voice still boomed rudely and noisily wherever I was.

"Now, this is my covenant..."

It must have been several hours, or several days later, I could not count the period of my captivity. Tired, hungry and abandoned, I beheld my captor as he slowly materialised from the darkness of unconsciousness. This time he looked like a true man of God, decked in regalia of white trousers and overcoat to match. His neat stockings, shoes and necktie were impeccably white

"You shall not be a rebel to my cause anymore; you shall be my newest prophet of the millennium."

That gave me quite a start. The metamorphosis of prophets was indeed miraculous even for dissidents. Yet what had just come from this new barrel of neck, robust set of cheeks and heavily indulged lips seemed quite in character. Nothing must come by dint of work or merit except by the caprice of the lord himself. Was this not how his hierarchy jostled tirelessly to curry favours, I could imagine. But then I was laughing.

"Is this another miracle?"

Babul showed his teeth in an angry snarl, the beast underneath his stylish appearance wanting to tear to open. But he won't let it yet.

"You must teach the faith," he went on, ignoring my irreverent question. "Your role will be to gather them, many more disciples and masses who will be looking to you. They are groping in their minds for a few explosive tickets to health, wealth and power, and you have the tricks. Tricks are necessary if you must gain a stable following, you know?"

But I was silent.

My silence must have meant my consent, for Babul then adjusted himself to appear more solidly in a grand seat ornamented with circular mirrors. Copious silvery lining trapped flaming red lights and threw angry fireworks around the corners. He leaned a bit closer to whisper conspiratorially and I shrank involuntarily from the deathly chill which exuded from his embodiment.

"You know, I was going to add unto you the legacy of Pastor Chris. He did his bit very well and now he's gone, blown up by a disgruntled church member, isn't that rather sad?

"They said he preached too many fearful sermons," he continued. "Well, now, those chilly waves of fear among the flock was power, you know?

"But I understand you want to teach peace, asalam, or whatever. We must add to them the comfort of a permanently witless state of consciousness. I will explain:

"There is a drawn battle for the mind of this world. Some old men who refuse to die - those compromisers of first disorder who can't just keep their mouths shut - have been spreading their message of liberty, just like you do with your counter tales: throwing words around, and quite a few are picking up these seeds in their heart.

"Now you will preach unity and faith, peace and progress, but read my lips: that four-footed creature draws from my mind which controls every behaviour on this soil with robotic precision.

"Negate and convict them, persuade them to repudiate their worth; immobilise, demobilise and leave them stagnated in the contradictions of their doctrines and injunctions. Lead them to lie here by my feet.

"The great lie is their loyalty; the more ignorant the more loyal to the cause; the more fanatical and violent...

"No, no I can see you are confused again," Baba waved his hands in the face of his frightened captive - being myself - who watched his every movement like a wary bird.

"Now let's put it this way. As your lord, I ask you: what are those other faces of my peace and harmony but your violence and wars; of my love and service but your competitions and hatred for one another? Your free will has overrun or contributed to overturn every good for the ascendancy of mediocrity within the entire fabric of all nations: Simple quantum leveller, don't you think?

"Your founding fathers did the same.

The Oracle

"Others are doing it everywhere.

"We are the hydra of every age on this soil.

"And all I am saying is lead - lead them on; carve a following. But teach these in verses and that great singing and dancing for which you are famous. And, with the powers I shall add to it, you might become the youngest prophet to razz the hunger of this age."

"But I will tell you again, young man, to beware of sabotage: you tend to seek the moral behind my tale," he leaned forward with a leer and shoved white-gloved claws in my face. "Now your lord cannot preside over the sabotage of his power, can he?"

I inwardly recoiled realising that what he actually meant by moral was truth. But cutting into his loathsome monologue, I blurted out: "I won't!"

The two words seemed to jar him for he started briefly. Then the dangerous gleam appeared in his eyes again.

"You won't? You mean turn again, tiger, against my will?" Babul growled. "Then I will damn you to hell. I will sit and preside over the radius of the brimstone that will consume you forever. You must understand, boy. East or west, the show must go on!

"Whether you want it or not!" he was roaring now like an angry lion.

Then there was silence.

His was the final, ominous threat, while mine was in contemplation of the complex paradox that gave rise to such a nightmare of human imagination. Or was it the silence of my own confounded grip by a titan who bestrode the human will with his awesome power and abuse of it? I could not tell…

II

Coming to think of it now, I could still have been under the dominion of that awful creature's mind if I had not met Nagua and held his rescue present in my palms.

Nagua's gift was in the form of an ancient, loose bound note he called my memory. "Within these pages," he had told us before we parted, "will be found every forgotten bits and pieces of your universe of dreams.

"And you can only so truly seek as to begin to remember again."

When I leafed through the pages, bold letters began to ring in soft gentle peals:

-One day we would return to the beginning of it all in the great continuum of being...

Those were weird and wonderful words I'd never heard before at the start of any story. And on the page was a familiar angel looking resplendent and full of life. She had on a silk cotton dress that covered her neck; her eyes were bright as were her lips from which flowed phrases that sounded inaudible but incredibly beautiful. I flipped the leaves as her words came alive:

-There are many parts to everything that happens any moment, any time...

-Parts untold, unfelt and unappreciated...

Each page unlocked a memory that expanded and lighted my quest beyond all I ever thought possible. I went on randomly till coming to the ending lines:

-Ours is to part the blinds and help our minds to glimpse these parts in their wholeness...

I was vaguely aware of a sigh that heaved through my whole frame. Finally, Nagua had brought me away from the control and haze of darkness into the memory of my secret selves. It felt like the rousing of one life breath after another. An intrinsic part of my being, for once, felt real and true. It had taken just one brief moment to come into the awakening. Henceforth a good head was mine to carry and protect. And neither panic nor mortal fear could fall upon it again.

But it does seem like I'm telling it all in reverse mode, doesn't it?

The Oracle

Now, to how I met Nagua...

Babul had left me cowed, beaten, hungry and desperate. He had made it clear I was his prey; I would do anything he wanted in order to live or survive the harrowing ordeal of slavery and punishment in that dense dungeon he had created for rebels of his art, as he tagged me and my kind. But no sooner had his presence withdrawn from view than I began to scan my mind for an escape route. Freedom, sweet freedom, was all I breathed; was all I lived and could ever hope for...

Soon there came a sound like the soft humming of celestial bees, coming in from the asphyxiating deep, that dense silence that mortally terrified a soul. My mind was like a malfunctioned clock working slowly backward, then reeling dizzily anti clockwise. Yet listening to the droning, and so considerably dulled, I felt being gently, ever so gently, drawn out of all premonitions.

I saw a pair of legs in canvas shoes fleeting across the air in quick, determined motions. Those were my legs...

Then I went numb as the legs leapt high up and landed on the dust. I tried to jump but too late! I came down with a heavy thud. Something like a canister hit my head. The fumes hissed directly under my nose. Another. Then another.

I scrambled to my feet, lungs and eyes stinging, my face smarting painfully. In the haze, I caught a glimpse of hooded figures edging after me. Babul's mad dogs! I spat and coughed violently. It felt like hell as more canister balls rained down.

Dazed, I ran harder. My lungs were threatening to burst. Then I burst through a thicket. There was my college hostel quarter... Or was it the female wing? Then there was ...infinity!

"You have returned?" Mma asked.

I quickly awoke to an airy, dreamy place where everything changed. There was no monster masquerade, no bull chase and the nightmarish struggles.

There was only the beautiful angel whose fragrance of morning rose lit all the centres within me. A serenade was singing somewhere in my heart.

Mma was that familiar angel. I remembered how we parted ways a long time ago in not too happy circumstances. Now all I wanted was speak gentle words to her and not the callous abandonment of the past. But I couldn't quite get them together. How would she take anything I said again? My heart thumped uncertainly.

Strangely she seemed without emotion. There was neither pride nor indignation in her voice, just the question which both of us knew the answer.

We were sitting side by side on a brown footstone under a low pine tree which whistled softly and endlessly. The sun was a pink, soft glow that blended gently with the azure hue of the clouds drifting so leisurely and lowly overhead that we could reach out and feel them in our hands. So close was everything, like the wind that rustled the pines. I could reach out to all things in this world by simply thinking of their beauty. There was an intimacy in everything that filled all space. I seemed to know many things yet there were so many things I was still to learn.

My apology tumbled jerkily. "I wronged you, Mamma," I tenderly began. "I came to say sorry for leaving you the way I did. That's hardly how we are meant to treat each other."

Yet, in spite of the peace and harmony around us, the words stuck in my throat. I felt like a prodigal who didn't deserve the welcome embrace. But Mma brushed this aside with a wave and the words: "No need for all that." She reached out to prod the soft soil, scooping a handful of brown, yellow sand to let them sift gently though her parted fingers. "Do you know where we are, Sun?" she called me in that affectionate manner she shortened my name. We cannot be sorry for the past; it's useless in the moment of truthful answers," she said.

The Oracle

"I'm not clinging to our misdeeds," I countered lamely. "But to correct them in order to move on with our lives..."

Her laughter rang out in the clear lustre of the pink sunshine interrupting my words. "What's there to correct when all is well within you? You always think in terms of wrong. But all is right here and now that brings us joy and beauty."

I looked at her wonderingly. This was a new girl in such a short time. She was more sanguine than I had known her to be. Her youth and beauty shone with the disinterestedness which seemed to underline her confidence and strength. It was like the strength of a panther.

She must have caught my thoughts and was rather bemused. "You see, you left for your mission and then I found the oracle. I found Nagua."

"Nagua," I repeated. "Who is Nagua?"

Then it dawned on me. Mma had a new man in her life. A surge of emotion shot through me. Here, I thought, was I reunited finally with my life's dream and she was talking about another with such daintiness and sheer delight. But Mma laughed, throwing away sand from her hands and rising simultaneously to her feet. "Isn't it beautiful," she exclaimed, "the loneliness of this world and the companionship of your soul."

The wind was rising softly, an invisible being that could only be felt and heard as sound. So was the rustling of the pine tree. Here was a silent land, spread-eagled, like an endless wild, and coloured with the unreality of pink majestic energy from the still overhead sun. "Come let's play," she called to me and without looking back, bounded gracefully into a low flowery brush.

I watched her for a few seconds, envying the joy and freedom of her every movement, the nimbleness of her body and the ease with which she glided in the air, hands spread out, beautiful round legs slightly poised for balance, and then it struck me how evenly balanced she was in our world. The more I watched her, the more it stirred in me an inner power, the strength to move, to forgo everything past and move into the fullness of living expression.

"Come," Mma's voice wafted close. My body rose in full vigour, yet I was unsure of my steps, trying to find my balance as my left leg caught in the sand and my right slipped, and my hands flailed briefly, a novice at the play.

Then letting go my attention on myself to concentrate on the élan form before me, I was soon sailing effortlessly, cutting through the moaning wind spirits whose sound had heightened to a still, vibrating drone. I sped and the sun's brilliance spread out to me her warm embrace of freedom and joy as I flung in the soft, pliant arms of my twin flame. Our union brought her gentle giggles in my face. A halo was spreading over her head. "How do you feel now?" she sang in the sound of the irrepressible wind.

"I feel I have everything I need here in my arms. You feel the same?"

She laughed in answer.

"And do I have that light on my head too?" I pointed. I was joyous and excited at the experience I was having in this wondrous corner of the universe.

"If you can feel it, then you have it," she teased.

And sure enough I could feel a dancing and glowing around my face and head and cheeks, and all over my body. It was all around me like a huge globe. I stretched my hands and light beams flashed out in colours of white and blue and yellow. Mma joined and soon we were sending multicolour lightning crisscrossing in great waves in the skies. I threw a dart at her which she deftly deflected with a bright beam. "Defend yourself!" she declared as we parried darts. "I am Imamma, the golden breasted one. And you?"

I paused, and her beam caught my shoulder blade, knocking me flat to the ground. I reeled in pain.

Mma laughed. "It's only your mind," she told me. "Nothing really hurts here, inside the memory of your worlds."

Then I stopped, transfixed by the most incredible vision I ever saw. The beings of the universe!

Hovering close above, around and within, they were strangely familiar faces. I recognised them all: fathers, mothers, grandfathers and stepmothers, aunts and uncles, great uncles and a host of friends and relations I never recalled existed before. I knew them now, the ancients of days from across all races of the known and unknown cosmos.

These were my ancestors, our higher companions who watched over us, silently, quietly always there in the background of all things, all events, nurturing and ever so gently, bringing us closer into the fuller realisation of our purpose in this world. These were my universal family! And they were calling my name in the softest, gentlest notes of music. "Kusun!" I announced with great delight, leaping like a teen who had just found the solution to a life long puzzle. "I am Kusunku of the orange sun!"

The proclamation had come with miraculous healing power, the last serene blast in the universal awakening. I was like one for whom a bad spell had been broken; a violent downpour had ended, the clouds had receded and I could see clearly for the first time in a long while.

I sat down to savour this silent thrill of recovery. Mma drew closer, placing a gentle hand around my neck, and announcing in her quaint, soft manner: "I welcome you to the meeting of me and you, Sun of my flaming heart!"

I could only smile as she stretched her hand to me. I took it and she pulled me up my feet. "Come let's wait. The search is nearly over. "For Nagua."

I felt an old dull ache return, and we were back under the pine tree, sitting side by side, our knees drawn up with our hands clasped over them. After a long time had passed with the girl's squinting and searching into the distance, I asked again. "Mamma, who is Nagua?"

Mma narrowed a pair of bright, intelligent eyes that were scanning the horizon as if expecting something to turn up there that very moment. "You know, there are times," she said without looking in my direction, "that you sound like I will understand you full well only when we have returned finally to that great continuum of being."

"Why is that?" I asked sheepishly.

"If you often act from the mind of fear and separation," her eyes flashed a sudden brilliant light, "you lose the courage and freedom of your deepest heart within?"

Her radiant white gleamed softly, tenderly. Her twinkle was there, faintly though, with a softness which bore compassion flowing like a spring. I clasped my arms around her neck, trusting and melting completely in the warmth of her being.

Presently she exclaimed. "There's Nagua! He's coming our way." And she was off in a quick sprint.

I followed her beautiful legs flitting nimbly across the rich ochre coloured soil toward a shadowy outline. As we drew close I could see that the figure looked strangely familiar in his bright white top and dark hued trousers. And when he turned to meet us, I realised with a jolt of surprise how foolish I had been to entertain doubts about the girl.

Nagua was no other than the glorious old fellow by the fireside, the greatest bard that ever lived in the Kongo tribe of Omaha and the whole region of Naigon: Onku himself!

So that was how I met Nagua...

And how I finally came to summon courage and seize the tale that had fooled the vain and meek. I was now ready for the final chapter. The final wakening, Nagua had said, was to confront the evil master, himself, face to face at his own demesne in the discarnate realm.

Crossing the earthly line and entering the fringe of the nether world was like delving in a moving screen where fuzzy shapes and dull colours were thrown before the vision in random black and white. The weird gurgling and howling of captive souls assailed your hearing, and the dizzy flight of life forms added to the horrendous illusion while you steadied your balance on the narrow path. One step out of turn was all it took to fall back into a warring world where you battled to break free from the tyranny of materialism and confusion.

And so with care and courage, I treaded. That was sure way to track the self acclaimed lord of the realm. I had to confront him at last with the secret he had hidden for so long from his human slaves. Because no longer was I his quarry. I was past the fear and awe that had paralysed the world for many, many generations.

A spiral of smoke from the conclave made it easy to locate the chimney residence. The approach was strangely unguarded save for few shadow energies that took form every now and then, trying to dig into your fears and grab at your mind. Babul knew few earthmen could summon the courage to journey out of their bodies, past the tunnel of terror and the shadow of death, to venture here where he fed from the energy of billions he had won to himself in worship and devotion.

Well, I may have been his fodder for some time but, unlike most, an unwilling one. For the matter had complicated further. The weaver of vanities had swallowed the ruse of his own omnipotence in the literal sense of the fable and had proven too complacent to credit anyone else with little intelligence. He had become the tortoise who thought he had all the wisdom of the world inside his personal calabash. Now a surprise awaited him.

I edged on gingerly, ignoring the hazardous motions around and without. Babul's minions.

They were prancing in and out and poking mischief on my vision. Formless and lurid, manifested by vile thoughts, they sought outlets in the depressing miasma of any mind open to them. But now I was filled with great courage, I could tell where his power lurked, digging his forays onto our souls, and manifesting as fast as our pitiful thoughts of our own unworthiness attracted him. I waved aside a green faced one brandishing a weapon in my face. It fell back into the shadows with a puff!

The thick grey cloud of mist around the hearth soon became a circle of dull red walls at whose tiny entrance stood waB the daemon. Beside this loyal servant at the gate was a green faced female who seemed impervious to the lewdness around her with waB massaging her fleshy derriere while she gave excited grunts and an empty look in space.

Then my eyes met his.

The hound leader was wearing his beastly hooded visage and a red band around his snout. This time he was genial in his greeting. "Here we are," he nodded, his hand dropping lazily to his side, "watching out for you, just in case."

This last line was a lie. In a way, he was saying he knew I would be coming here at this very moment and he was just standing by to receive me. waB had grown into the dissembling that went with the art. It kept the audience in awe believing that the priest, like God, knew everything that would happen at any crucial moment in the lives of his devotees. But that was another ruse of the text.

Deftly he motioned the woman to hold on. She was somehow sheep staring at me with naked desire and chewing frantically on what must be flesh gums in her mouth.

"Follow me," he turned, leading the way, still not resisting the urge to lay his hands around that derriere in a parting gesture. Then he hobbled forward like a silhouette in twilight. His dirty whiskers bristled in the dull grey smoke; his eyes darted left and right. Finally, he made a noise as if to throw up sputum or something worse. Then he seemed to think otherwise and gave a short, uneasy laugh.

"That day of the chase was nothing personal; just orders," he began. "Surely, as one of us, you must understand."

The Oracle

I gave him silence as we clumped through a decrepit hallway covered with dirty, slivery soot and webs. Everything here fell in with the depressing stockpile of smoke and mirrors that threw multiples of images all around the corners.

"Man, I am so relieved to have you back. I can't tell you how terrible it was to fight a fellow brother in the cause. Anyhow," he sounded almost apologetic, "with our eyes on our permanent interests, your enemy today might just be your friend tomorrow."

"That open secret," I replied indifferently, "Isn't it the cornerstone of your lies?"

waB gave a short, uneasy laugh.

"You have a strange sense of humour, man. There's nothing we have that you seem to care for. Even our dos don't seem to hold water with you. Let alone our don'ts."

I shook my head. "Not any more. When you see the trick of the tale, you are bound to a wake up call."

"Trick of the tale!" he gave an uncertain smirk. "I can see why everyone told Baba you could be the ruin of us. Your ideas will do away with everything we cherish so much? Now that's close to heresy. A tale isn't just a tale when we have loyal members for its cause ...um um", he cleared his throat on a conciliatory note. "Everything you see here is... personal, you know. Can't be too discreet though about our privacy, can we?" Now he was sounding strangely rhetorical.

"Isn't that the ruin of us?" I smiled back to him. "Don't worry, you are none of my business; you never were. After all, you are my kinsman, waB," I assured him.

He grinned back, not understanding my meaning but blurting in his mechanical manner. "Who knows, one day, we could even become first cousins by his lordship...

"Now here is His Holiness, Babul the Greatest, Conqueror of the world," cried the priest daemon, suddenly bowing very low.

He sat on a high stool decked with the dull glitter of red and silvery stones. The blood-red hood covered from his huge shoulders to his toes. You could visualise any primeval lord hunched in a high seat, the giant mirrors adding to his imposing size as he glowered down to his subjects below, and that would be the beast himself.

Babul was flanked by over a hundred high priests of his inner sanctum. They were dressed in their ceremonial crimson hoods, holding dim lighted objects in each hand which caught the mirrors and threw gleams around a dome that slanted dangerously above. He gave a satisfied nod to his priest and began to sniff the air around me. "You come to me with courage. But I see vexation in your eyes," he began.

I smiled quizzically and he drew a blank.

He tried another angle. "Congratulations, young man, you have made it. Are you not honoured to be counted among the highest of my realm? This is a great occasion in your life."

"Great indeed," I interrupted, aware of the slight frown of disapproval from his hood as I walked straight up the raised dais on which he sat. It happened in seconds, too quickly for his expectation. It brought muffled gasps of surprise from his congregation.

"Now get your zombies out of sight. I want to speak to you alone," I began in a calm, determined voice. "In your own interest, Babul," I added, "for you won't like them to hear what I have to say, I assure you."

Babul was taken aback. But one look into my eyes decided for him. He waved a left to his men and, in a minute, the rigid, immobile order of psychic moguls disappeared through hidden doors in the wall. I glanced around a few seconds to be sure. Even the daemon waB was nowhere to be seen.

"Good," I began, "I guess you know by now why I will neither serve nor be herdsman of your force in any way."

"You gave me your silent agreement," Babul snarled. He was clearly exasperated by what was becoming my merry go round with him on the subject of tending his slaves on earth. "When you put your hands on my plough, there's no going back!" his voice became a bellow that resounded with loud echoes in the open debris of his kingdom.

But I was unperturbed. The story was winding full circle in his face and you had to get used to the twin aspects of this conquering lord. The benign face he might reserve to loyal worshippers under his aura but the demonic visage was what he welded against any who dared doubt on some matters of contradiction in his ways. This time I couldn't give a whiff for either.

"It's not my fault how you interpret silence. Listen," I stared into his self indulgent snout, "and I will tell this story..."

"Oh ho, you own the tale now," he laughed in derision but he was uneasy as far as I could sense the chill around him.

"That part we don't know yet is a tale that must be told, my friend."

"Oh ho, I'm now your friend," Babul scorned again. "You never called me that before, did you?" his face puckered with rage. "I am your lord!" he made that reverberating bellow again.

"And master," I retorted. "Now listen. A long, long time ago, there were two brothers. And there was a crime. Surely you will recall what one did to the other."

I sensed Babul freeze.

"Drink the blood, eat the flesh.

"Steal a mind; sell your soul.

"Anything for power and glory over the earth.

"And the smoky world of hell...

"Shouldn't you be asking to know this interloper?" I interrupted myself.

He was very still.

I continued. "Give the name and the spell is broken.

"A little drop of truth, a million tons of lies. Isn't that how you spin the wheel?"

Babul's face had turned the colour of ash in wet dew. "What do you mean by these silly riddles?" he sneered.

"Who owns the story, Baba? The weaver of myths -

"The millions who bow and clap their hands?

"Or the greed that only wants more and more?

"Now, what made the moral disappear like a mist in the rising sun?"

"I see you've been dreaming," Babul began.

"But it is all a dream, Barwa," I called his given name. "Two hundred years of the myth that fed your power."

For a second I thought my eyes were deceiving me. The great lord was sweating profusely.

"There's only one trouble in your book, Babul: You underrate who we are inside -

"And overrate your own image in the mirror."

"You can't..." Babul practically choked like he was about to have a heart attack.

"Can't I?" I pressed on. "While you worked every angle of our ignorance, you never bargained for the other force - the light of awakened souls beaming up the universe."

"See how you dare the anger of your lord!" Although Babul's voice was thundering everywhere within his dilapidated mansion, I had seen his desperation and that was the confirmation I needed.

"You were disembodied a long time," I countered. "They call you lord; you're no more lord than these things by the smoky way..."

Then I relented with a shrug of indifference. Babul now knew that I also knew what he thought only him knew above everyone else. I had made my point on his origins and it was time to leave.

"Keep your hood and tell your slaves the truth, Babul. They will love you still. And when they wake up becomes their morning. Bye for now. I can find my way out."

He was beaten.

Babul was down but not completely out, mind you. His final act would depend on the millions riveted upon his magic. Would they dare to look behind the drapery of his fiction? Would they follow their intuition or just a tale for its own sake? Would they find within their inner being the answers they sought, or depend on priests and tyrants for half truths that demean their souls? It was up to them. As for me, I had woken from a deep slumber where forgetfulness dwelled. Now I was ready to savour the beauty of hearts awake.

At the doorway, Babul called to me, "Friend," for the first time. I turned.

His horrid paws were folded across his chest. He looked deflated, the pride and arrogance almost gone. "I didn't kill my little brother," he said. "It was he who gave up his life."

That was a new version.

"They said you were twins," I replied. But the usurper brushed that one aside.

"He gave up his life for me. Willingly, like all those who come to me, you see?"

I smiled. "Another half-truth," I replied, "but I shall pass."

Cousin waB was waiting for me by the hallway and snuffling his damsel, the greyhound woman, by the side. "It is done?" he hazarded as he turned to lead the way out.

"It is done," I replied doubtfully.

The daemon leader betrayed no emotion; he was playing the game of knowing things before hand, their theatrics in divine omniscience. But then one thing was certain between us: we were past the time of muscles flexed and fangs bared against each other. For with fear and uncertainty gone now, he too knew the sign of the end when the audience no longer answered eagerly 'Yes, Yes!' to the call of 'Story, Story!! '

He parted the smoking blind to let me step past.

And in his mind I could read the dilemma of the art that enslaved him and his fellows. Here was their only tale of dread and might. Better to revel in a dream that promised everything they could want than the truth that shook them rudely and with no titles to their little selves. So, I thought, let it be a deep sleep for them that might never rouse awake.

At that point, waB paused to let me walk on through the chimney smoke that spiralled from the mouth of the gigantic coven that led to the borderline of the earthly realm.

"And now, each to his own woman, NwaBala," I called his full name. He barely managed to contain his jolt at that one. "Look now unto your house, isn't it how it's said?"

"I mustn't forget that piece of bone wisdom," waB replied with a wink, stepping gingerly backward to his female company.

I was left alone to pick my way through the thickening flux, past the noises of life starved creatures. Half in and out of my mind, I kept wondering how-

How the likes of Babul could ever have counted to the many forever groping in the shadows of mighty dreams...

It nearly proved a costly mistake letting my mind wander. There was hardly a warning before it dropped -a devastating dart that paralysed the senses and brought me instantly to my knees.

Babul!

I had underrated the con artist again, and history was about to laugh for the umpteenth time. Why did I think he would let me out of his sphere without a fight?

Fool! I berated myself, to be annihilated by an underhanded cut, an exhumation of trickery and cowardice more sickening than this dense fog in this lowly graveyard.

Then I heard their gurgling: Babul's minions and their gibberish that mortified and made stupor of the mind.

They were tearing the life force from me, to dissipate my energy in slavish duties. I would become a nameless cipher among those millions of zombies.

I was going to die!

The realisation stampeded me to action. I began a desperate struggle to defend myself, commanding, holding back the psychic attack, pushing against the onslaught on my existence...

The Oracle

It seemed like aeons.

Bravely I stood my ground.

And soon began to feel their claw holds weakening.

Gasping, I filled my lungs with vibrant energy currents of the spheres. I gently asked the blessed forces to enliven the invisible centres within me.

That was when I saw the light. In my desperation had I forgotten the great moral to bravely light up the world on a moment like this.

I began to visualise it, to feel it coursing, steady and unwavering, through my whole ethereal form.

It seemed an infinite length of effort and action.

Then I felt it more the very next time.

Like a gentle wave of energy, forming through a grey veil, a tiny blob, almost weak and imperceptible against the blindfold and paralysis of hell...

It came breaking out!

Without warning, letting a piercing keynote which coursed the length and breadth of the darkened void, its motion, unparalleled in power, burst forth, obliterating all in its way.

The streaks of heavenly fire scoured lovingly, and fiercely.

And in the next instant, I, Kusunku, caught in the wing of the heavens, was swirling up, and up, as a blinding sheet.

Then I was wide alert.

*

Under the mango tree, it was still noon but seemed to be morning yet.

Komas was laughing heartily at me. "Man, you look like you saw the ghost of Barwa himself! Don't tell me Onku's monster gave you the boo-boo chase."

Our uncle had an amused expression while he regarded me with a sly grin. Perhaps he was wondering if he had opened a head with his tale today, I mused only briefly.

"Did you find what you seek or has my story scared the life of you?" he teased.

I roused myself to reply evenly: "You know, it's no longer your story now, Onku."

I could still remember a little and was trying to reconcile some of what happened with the familiar reality that had jerked me to wakefulness. The fire had burnt out. Only the ashes and debris remained. Onku's pipe, too, was spent and now rested within easy reach of his hand beside a footstool. I imagined it waiting for another moment to perform that subtle feat into the mystery of an untold tale.

"The story is mine as well," I told him. "And I am going to do with it... what I have to do with it."

"No teasing, son of Eva," Onku laughed. "I think I've opened one head at last. And, sooner than I thought, the bird readies to soar to the realms of ancient gods."

I did not understand his last cryptic verse. But it felt good to know the story was ours to remember and, perhaps, one day, tell as deemed fit to some others willing to hear. I too had become an inheritor in the line of the eagle clan.

Chin Ce

*

Chin Ce falls in the category of younger African poets whose works have gained some critical attention for their expressive power and originality of thought. Nigerian-born and educated at Calabar, Ce has given his time to Africa, travelling and taking notes in an enterprise that includes teaching, journalism and literature.

Like most poets of his generation Chin Ce began writing poetry at college where 'The Cow Chase,' his first poem, was presented in the Calabar Elsa Press. Maturing in an era of frequent military interventions in the political life of the Nigerian people Ce began writing political poetry, his influences drawn from or matching the canons of modern thinkers like Fanon, Deleuze and Lévinas.

Children of Koloko, his first work of fiction, was written in the hoary eighties of Nigeria's history. It was however published two decades later in 2000. In succession came *Gamji College* (2001). His latest fiction *The Visitor* appeared in 2004 followed by *Millennial* (2005), his third volume of poetry which he dedicates to the rising awareness in humanity ('All That Is') in an age of extreme ignorance among the world's poor.

Prior to these *An African Eclipse* had appeared in 1999 while *Full Moon*, his second collection of poems, was published 2001, which go to confirm what a critic had noted of his works as seamless temporal movements in the psychological order of the writer's private and public domain.

Chin Ce who has been most critical of the entire Nigerian history of anti-people legacies is a writer of intense vision. Anything may be inferred from his rather pessimistic dismissal of the Nigerian state as 'the buffoonery of the millennium' in the essay 'Bards and Tyrants,' and his glowing notes for Ghana among the West African nations. His renunciation is however not in the tradition of exile common with Nigerian nationals fleeing a country for the reason that nothing of decency -from electricity and communication to their transportation systems- can ever work under the series of corrupt leadership prevailing there. On the contrary Ce is always in his home country to cohort with family members and take care of matters of business.

Selected Bibliography

Other Works by Chin Ce

Fiction

Children of Koloko (2001)
Gamji College (2002)
The Visitor (2004)
The Oracle (2013)
The Dreamer (2013)
African Short Stories (Edited) 2013

Poetry

An African Eclipse (1999)
Full Moon (2001)
Millennial (2005)

Essays

Bards and Tyrants: Literature, Leadership and Citizenship Issues of Modern Nigeria (I)
Bards and Tyrants: Literature, Leadership and Citizenship Issues of Modern Nigeria (II)
A Dance of the Ether: Four Decades of African Poetry in English
A Griot of his Time: Chinweizu in Contemporary African Poetry
The Art of the Younger Poets: Assertions and Changing Paradigms.
The Art of the Younger Poets: Frontliners and Visionaries
The Art of the Younger Poets: Love, Nature and Sweet Remembrances
Mutant Traditions: Welcoming the International Council
Beyond the Word: And the truth we now so well
Of Dreams, Memory and Imagination
Happily After: Re-visioning African writing
Riddle me': The Creative Wit of Alaa's Children (I)
Bash them': The Creative Wit of Alaa's Children (II)
Igbo Mind: Music, Culture and Religion (I)
Igbo Mind: Music, Culture and Religion (II)
And Tortoise Flew
A Story of Courage
A Teacher's Art
Close Strangers
Unending Narratives
Critics of the New Poetry

160

SELECTED CRITICISM

Cope, J. S. and K. Chester. 'Stealing the White Man's Weapon or Forging One's Own? African and African-American English in Ce's *Children of Koloko* and Morrison's *Beloved*' *Critical Supplement: The Works of Chin Ce*. Ed. Irene Marques, Ircalc, 2007

De La Cruz-Guzmán, Marlene. 'Bi-living, Time and Space: LeAnne Howe's *Shell Shaker* and Chin Ce's *The Visitor.*' *Across Borders: African Literature and Culture* No.7. 2010.

Eke, Kola. 'Closer to Wordsworth: Nature and Pain in Chin Ce's *Full Moon Poems*' *Critical Supplement: The Works of Chin Ce*. Ed. Irene Marques, Ircalc, 2007.

Emezue, GMT. 'Chin Ce and the Postcolonial Dialogue of Gamji College' *Critical Supplement (A) 1: The Works of Chin Ce*. Ed. Irene Marques, Ircalc, 2007

- - -. The Cean Dialogues. *Africa and Her Writers*. JALC 10 Special Edition, Morrisville: Lulu Press, 2013

Grants, Amanda. 'Memory, Transition and Dialogue: The Cyclic Order of Chin Ce's Oeuvres.' *Re-Imagining African Literature* vol. II, Morrisvile: ARI, 2006.

Hamilton, G. A. R. 'Beyond Subjectificatory Structures: Chin Ce 'In the season of another life.' *Critical Supplement: The Works of Chin Ce*. Ed. Irene Marques, Ircalc, 2007.

Marques, Irene. 'The Works of Chin Ce: A Critical Overview' *Critical Supplement: The Works of Chin Ce*. Ed. Irene Marques, Ircalc, 2007

Okuyade, Ogaga. 'Locating the Voice: The Modernist (Postcolonial) Narrative Maze of Chin Ce's *The Visitor*' *Critical Supplement: The Works of Chin Ce*. Ed. Irene Marques, Ircalc, 2007.

- - -. 'Oral Collage, Multidimensional Perspectives in the Novels of Chin Ce, Phaswane Mpe and Biyi Bandele-Thomas.' *Oral Traditions: The Journal of African Literature* 6. 2009.

- - -. 'The Rhetoric of Despair in Chin Ce's Children of Koloko.' *A Widening Frontier*. Nairobi: WP, 2007.

Sanyal, D. 'Eco-critical Spaces: The Natural Landscape of New Nigerian Poetry.' *Critical Approaches* vol.2 AI: ABN: 2008.

- - -. 'Violence and Oral Metaphors in Chin Ce's *Gamji College*.' *War and Conflict,* Ircalc 2008.

Smith, Charles. 'For God and Country: Chin Ce *Millennial* Verses.' *Journal of New Poetry*, No. 8, 2008.

Sone, Enongene Mirabeau and Djockoua Manyaka Toko. 'Orature and Oratorical Teaching Strategies in African Literature: The Examples of Laye Camara and Chin Ce.' *A Widening Frontier*. JALC 4, 2007.

Toko, Djockoua Manyaka. 'Educating the Child with Camara Laye's *The Dark Child* and Chin Ce's *Children of Koloko*' *Critical Supplement: The Works of Chin Ce*. Ed. Irene Marques, Ircalc, 2007.

Usongo, Kenneth. 'Pedagogy of Disillusionment: The Case of Ferdinand Oyono's *The Old Man and the Medal* and Chin Ce's Chin Ce's *Gamji College.' Critical Supplement (A) 1: The Works of Chin Ce*. Ed. Irene Marques, Ircalc, 2007.